Praise for Larissa Ione's *Snowbound*

"Great voice, GREAT characters!"

~ *USA Today bestselling author Jill Shalvis*

"This sexy little story takes the gold."

~ *Coffee Time Romance*

5/5 Angels! "Larissa Ione creates lovely characters... This is one outstanding book that is marvelously crafted."

~ *Fallen Angels Reviews*

"Snowbound is an emotional story that is not so much about the sex as it is about the romance. ...The romance is emotional, tender and sensual in its intensity. ...Snowbound is a well crafted example of the power of love over adversity and is well worth the time and money spent. Bravo, Ms. Ione."

~ *Lettetia Elsasser, eCataromance*

Snowbound

Larissa Ione

A SᴀᴍhᴀIN PᴜᴏʟIshING, Lᴛᴏ. publication.

Samhain Publishing, Ltd.
577 Mulberry Street, Suite 1520
Macon, GA 31201
www.samhainpublishing.com

Snowbound
Copyright © 2008 by Larissa Ione
Print ISBN: 978-1-59998-823-8
Digital ISBN: 1-59998-608-6

Editing by Anne Scott
Cover by Dawn Seewer

First Samhain Publishing, Ltd. electronic publication: September 2007
First Samhain Publishing, Ltd. print publication: July 2008

Dedication

Snowbound, though one of my early works, has always been special to me, sort of "the book of my heart". It deals with subject matter with which I've been more intimate than I'd like. For that reason, I have two very special dedications. First, to my step-nephew, Sean, after whom the hero, Sean Trenton, is named. An Army Ranger who died too young, Sean lived life to the fullest, just like the hero. This is for you, kiddo.

And to my husband, Bryan, who fought the hero's battle and won, but not without paying a price. I love you, baby.

Chapter One

"What do you mean you're canceling?"

Robyn Montgomery seethed as she listened to her ex-boyfriend's lame excuses for backing out of the only commitment she'd ever asked of him. The fact that he was also her boss only compounded her anger.

She held the telephone handset in a death grip, thinking he could have told her the news in person when he'd stopped by the station headquarters this morning instead of calling from the radio station's promotion party for an up-and-coming rock band. But then, Damon had never been one for confrontation.

"Damn it, Damon." She lowered her voice so Lisa, the secretary across the hall, wouldn't hear. "This is more than just your ski vacation and my high school reunion. You'll be disappointing a lot of people. Mostly kids."

"Yeah, well, here's the thing," he began, and went on about his responsibilities as Chicago's most popular radio and TV personality, about how as a major stockholder in the international corporation that owned the station he was expected at some upcoming events, and about how...well, she didn't know. She'd stopped listening.

Eventually, he ran out of excuses, and she jumped in before he invented some more. "I know all of that is important to you, but this is important to me. Please don't do this." He said nothing, but the sound of him laughing with someone nearby rang in her ears. How nice that ruining her life didn't get in the way of his having fun. "Damon? Did you hear me?"

"Sure. Look, backing out is for the best. I'm just not into doing the whole auctioneer gig. I'll see you when you get back. Have a nice trip."

She could practically feel her blood pressure blow off the gauge, and she had to clench her teeth to keep from shouting. "You've changed, Damon. And not for the better." Hand shaking, she slammed down the handset. God, she was screwed.

"Robyn?" Lisa popped her purple-streaked blonde head through the doorway. "Do you want me to get Mr. Hardy on the phone for you now?"

"I'll do it later. He's probably not in on a Saturday, anyway." Robyn and Lisa shouldn't be, either, but with a major cross-promo television-radio event coming up the day after Robyn was supposed to return from the reunion, they'd needed to put in some overtime.

Lisa frowned. "But Damon told me to make sure you—"

"Damon can wait," Robyn snapped, still furious and teetering on the verge of panic. But to be fair, none of this was Lisa's fault, so Robyn took a deep breath that did little to calm her. "I'm sorry. I promised I'd get him the interview with *Rolling Stone*, and I will."

But she'd take her sweet time. He didn't deserve any special effort after what he'd done to her. And what was he thinking anyway, asking the *secretary* to keep tabs on her? Robyn was the station's music director. *She* decided what music got played and what didn't. *She* handled the music library and promotional materials. Only three people outranked her. Of course, one of them was Damon.

"Okay." Lisa gave a bouncy shrug. "I'm going to lunch. Want anything?"

"No thanks. I'm not hungry." Big understatement. Her nerves had been rioting for a couple of weeks now, and Damon's little stunt was the icing on the cake she wasn't hungry for.

Lisa gave her abdomen an exaggerated pat. "Ditto. I noshed on way too many of those things you made."

"The *lebküchen*?"

"Uh-huh. You have to stop bringing in treats. I put on like, five pounds today."

If five pounds had gone on Lisa's model-thin body, Robyn didn't know where. Lisa glanced at the clock above Robyn's file cabinet. "If you change your mind about lunch, buzz my cell. Later!"

Ignoring the pile of administrative paperwork and the stack of music singles awaiting placement into station programming, Robyn swiveled her chair away from the desk and gazed out the twentieth-floor window. Freezing rain and wind. Typical Chicago winter weather.

Damon might have bailed on her, but she still had a plane ticket that would whisk her away from the never-ending gray days. Her hometown, a sprawling, modern mecca for the rich and famous that sat at the base of an internationally renowned ski resort, promised the perfect break. There was never a shortage of snow and sun. Even with twenty feet of snow on the ground, a person wearing shorts could sit outside and get a tan. Robyn had done that often as a child and even more often as a teen.

Not that having a winter tan had made any difference in how her classmates treated her. Or how she'd thought of herself. She wasn't sure how she felt about returning for the first time in years to the place where she'd been so miserable, but right now anything looked better than being in the same city with Damon.

"Hey, you."

Robyn grinned at the sound of her friend's voice. "I smell pizza." She spun the chair around, turning her back on the gloomy day and her gloomier thoughts.

Karen Hahn stood in the doorway with two cans of soda and a box from the ground-floor deli. "I had a craving, and no one makes a pie like Antonio."

"Ahh, Antonio," Robyn sighed dreamily. "Too bad he's gay."

"Maybe we could convert him." Smiling mischievously, Karen took a seat across the desk from her. "Though Damon might have something to say about your part in that."

Robyn snorted. "Like he cares. We haven't been together for anything more than dinner meetings in months." Which was fine with her. Sex with Damon had been a mostly one-sided experience—his side.

Karen opened the box, and Robyn's mouth watered at the sight of the pepperoni and fresh garlic pizza. Suddenly, she was famished.

"Maybe the trip will revive things. A little snow, a lot of steam...who knows what can happen?"

So much for the appetite. "Even if I wanted to revive things, which I don't, it wouldn't matter. He cancelled."

"But we fly out tomorrow!" Karen's gray eyes flashed as she lifted a slice from the box and piled the strings of gooey cheese on top. "That asshole. Honestly, I have no idea what you saw in him. I mean, besides his looks. He's way too full of himself."

"Oh, come on, admit it." Robyn plucked a pepperoni off the pizza and popped it into her mouth. Mmm, heaven. And *not* on her diet. "He wasn't a total jerk until he got that TV gig and turned all celebrity hotshot."

"I guess. But you still didn't need to make a devil's deal with him just so he'd help you out with the reunion. You can get another auction emcee, and you didn't need him as your date. You're a success with or without him."

"I know." Robyn blew out a frustrated breath. How could he have sunk that low? "But now that he's backed out of the charity auction, we're going to lose a lot of money and I'm going to look like the same bungling dork I was in high school."

Karen put down her pizza, and her normally cheery expression turned grim. "I've tried to keep my mouth shut about this—"

"You think I'm taking the reunion too seriously."

"Well, duh. I mean, come on. Those people don't matter anymore. You don't need to prove anything."

Robyn ate another pepperoni slice and chewed until she was ready to talk. Yes, she was going overboard, was being immature, even, but Karen would never understand. She hadn't been there, hadn't lived through what Robyn had.

"You were pretty and popular," she pointed out. "I couldn't even get a date for the school dances. How pathetic is that?"

"But you were smart."

Robyn rolled her eyes. "Which made me look like a loser who studied because I didn't have a social life."

And as a loser with no social life, she'd had few friends and had been teased unmercifully about her thick glasses, her frizzy red hair and acne, her weight, her utter lack of athletic ability...basically, if her classmates could tease her about something, they did.

None of them had expected her to move away from her family. None of them had expected her to grow out of her ugly, awkward stage and actually lose her virginity. None of them had expected her to become anything but an employee in her parents' bakery.

So she'd done the unexpected on all counts. And now, ten years later, she was ready to rub some noses in her success, to show she could climb the professional ladder to the summit and land the guy.

Except, now there was no guy. No fabulous dinner dates. No watching movies while snuggling on the couch. No mind-blowing orgasms that didn't involve a vibrator.

"I'm sure you're worrying for nothing." Karen cast Robyn a concerned glance. "He didn't do anything crazy like cancel our room, did he? We still have a place to stay?"

Robyn nodded and gave silent thanks that she herself had booked the room she and Karen were sharing at the ski lodge. Thanks to the upcoming ski competition and world snowboard championships, every hotel in the county would be full, and they'd have been forced to room with one of her siblings while her parents were remodeling their house. Talk about a nightmare. Her oldest brother, Greg, was a slob who decorated his walls with pickles from fast-food hamburgers, and Joe had so many roommates he needed a turnstile instead of a door.

"Good. Then Damon hasn't ruined everything." Karen pushed a can of cola across the desk to Robyn. "Just don't forget you promised you'd ski with me."

"You know I hate skiing." Well, she'd loved it as a child, but a lot had changed since then.

"I'm not letting you back out. Besides, it'll be good for you." Karen's eyes glinted with excitement. "Ooh, and now that Damon's out of the picture, we'll find some hunky ski guys to play hide-the-mitten with. We'll have a blast! You'll see. Snow, crackling fires, hot toddies—"

"Okay, okay," Robyn said, laughing. "I'm not sure about the hunky ski guy, but I'll make an effort to get on skis again. Just for you." She raised a curious eyebrow. "And I'm afraid to ask about hide-the-mitten."

Karen waved her hand dismissively. "We'll get a gorgeous man to help you out with that one. A fling with a hot non-celebrity will do you good. And I'm sure you'll find a last-minute replacement for the auction. You've got connections."

"I hope so, or I won't be able to show my face back home again."

The pizza in her stomach suddenly turned sour, and the panicky sensation she associated with failure gripped her like an icy band around her chest. Why hadn't she thought to secure a backup emcee in the event that something happened to Damon? Now it would to be next to impossible to find anyone else willing to volunteer their time, and paying someone wasn't an option.

But she'd do it. She had to. Besides, there was a bright side to all of this. "At least I won't have to spend the next two weeks with Damon."

No small relief there. They'd broken up months ago but had remained friends, and they'd made a deal. She'd been his no-strings date for business and social events despite the fact that she hated public life with all the schmoozing and falseness and women who threw themselves at Damon's feet. In return, Damon had agreed to escort her to the reunion party and to emcee the charity auction sponsored by her graduating class—a charity auction she'd been stupid enough to volunteer to organize.

Now it looked like she'd be dateless, emcee-less, and never free of her past. On the upside, she was free of egotistical celebrities.

Admittedly, that silver lining was paper thin, but at this point, she'd take what she could get.

✳ ✳ ✳

"Ski good or eat wood."

At the top of Suicide Run, Sean Trenton jammed his ski poles into the snow and squinted in the bright sunlight at his patrol partner. "What?"

"Ski good or eat wood," Todd repeated, pulling his goggles down over his eyes. "We were talking about Patrick on the lift up here. That's what he said. Right before he slammed into a tree and cracked a rib three years ago."

"No way."

"Yup."

Sean laughed. "Can't think of anyone who deserved it more."

"No doubt. The guy's an ass. Good thing he retired last year or we'd still be listening to his bullshit."

"Yeah," Sean said, smirking. "Now I only have to listen to yours."

Ignoring Todd's sputtering curse, he shoved off, cold air blasting his face as he shot down the slope. His K2s glided over the foot of fresh snow they'd gotten last night, scratching out quick turns and delivering bursts of speed in the straight lines.

God, he loved this. The biting sting of the wind, the smells of pine and fir and snow, the sound of his edges carving the ice. Life on the slopes was in his blood, his soul. He never felt more alive than when he was on skis. The moment he stepped out of his boots, the world bled out from Technicolor to fuzzy gray.

"We should be coming up on the victim!" he shouted back

to Todd. They'd been sent out after a snowboarder in possible trouble, and as Sean rounded a bend, the guy came into view.

He was sitting in a drift just off the run, his head lolling back against a tree. His board lay at an angle beside him. Sean braked a foot away in a spray of powder.

"Hey, buddy, you okay?" The mohawk-haired twenty-something started to push to his feet, but Sean placed a gloved hand on the guy's shoulder. "Stay still. If you're injured—"

"Oh, no, dude," the snowboarder replied in a California surfer drawl. "I stopped to take a leak. I needed a smoke after I drained the vein." He held up an extinguished cigarette butt. "No need to save me from a cracked head."

"I'd say we're a little late for that," Todd muttered, just loud enough for Sean to hear.

Ignoring his partner, Sean bent closer to the boarder. "You sure you're not hurt?"

The kid jumped to his feet and grabbed his board. "I'm cool. Thanks for checkin', though."

Todd radioed dispatch and notified them of the situation as the guy slid away.

"Wanna head in?" Sean asked, after Todd replaced the radio on his belt. "We're off the clock in a few minutes."

"Beat you to the lodge." And Todd was gone.

Cursing, he pushed off, his friend's challenge burning in his veins. Todd had some good moves and a head start, but Sean had speed and pro experience and not a small amount of recklessness going for him.

And he hated to lose.

A rush of adrenaline pumped into his system as he tucked and accelerated, heating his body, prickling his skin, his scalp. *Yes.* This was life, the high he lived for. The ultimate snowgasm.

15

Larissa Ione

Nothing compared; not money, not cars, not sex.

Well, maybe sex, but not lately.

The distance between Sean and his partner closed as he ripped turns and slammed over bone-jarring moguls. Oh, yeah. He was there. He took a jump and flew past Todd with a "see ya" wave.

At the bottom of the run he dug in his edges and slowed, careful not to wipe out any unsuspecting skiers. He slid across the flat through the crowd and arrived at the lodge with Todd on his heels.

"I'll beat you one of these days," Todd grumbled.

Sean peeled off his goggles and snapped out of his bindings. "Keep on dreaming."

They locked their skis and poles into a rack near the lodge wall and started up the steps to the ski patrol office, stomping their boots to break the snow loose. Sean tugged off his gloves and shoved them into his jacket pocket. "Want to hit the Moose and get something to eat?"

Todd glanced at his watch. "Sounds good. We can check out today's selection of ski babes. Get you out of your slump."

"Slump? Nah. Remember Jenny?"

"Dude, Jenny was *months* ago. And you had what, one date?"

One date that had ended in disaster, but no way in hell he'd tell Todd that.

"So it's been a while."

"A while? Monks get laid more often than you." Todd clapped Sean on the back as they entered the patrol office. "Don't worry. I'll get you back into prime playboy condition."

"Thanks, I think."

Todd grinned. "Shouldn't be a problem. Chicks fall all over

you even when they *don't* know who you are, and there've been hordes of hot women on the slopes lately."

"There always are before a ski competition." Always. Women came in droves hoping to land in one or more of the athletes' beds. He knew firsthand how it worked, had once considered groupies a perk of being the best of the best.

They punched their timecards and stowed their gear, and then clomped to the Moosehead Pub just off the cavernous main lobby. Six fires blazed in the tri-level, open-floor establishment, and he shivered as his body began to thaw after three solid hours on the slopes.

The bar was packed, but several barstools stood empty, so Sean and Todd took root at two that allowed the best view of the busy ski runs. The bartender, Earl, slapped napkins on the polished oak bar top.

"Hey, boys. What can I do ya for?"

"The usual," Sean said. "Cocoa and a burger."

"Coffee for me. Strong coffee." Todd raked his fingers through his shaggy blond hair. "I need some serious juice."

Sean raised an eyebrow. "Got a date?"

"I wish," Todd muttered. "I'm on duty at the station tonight."

"Man, I don't know how you manage two jobs."

"I can't afford to only do EMT work in the summer." Todd gave Sean a meaningful look. "Unlike some people."

He shot his friend an irritated glare. "Fuck you."

"Hey, I was joking."

Sean scrubbed a hand over his face. It didn't take much to set him off these days, which was unlike him. "I know."

"The new job got you wound up?"

"Like a watch," Sean said. "What if I screw up? The producers will never hire me on a permanent basis."

Todd rolled his eyes. "You're kidding, right? Who knows more about skiing than you? And once chicks see your mug on TV, you'll be the most popular sports commentator in history."

"We'll see."

"You're way too stressed. You gotta get laid."

Earl set two steaming mugs in front of them, and Sean poked idly at the marshmallows floating on top of his cocoa. His stomach was too knotted to eat now. Announcing the ski competition on national TV was an opportunity he couldn't afford to mess up.

Only it wasn't about the money; it was about putting his life back together, and the possibility that he might fail drove him crazy. He needed a distraction, a release, but Todd's insistence that the release be sexual in nature wasn't the answer.

Then again, maybe it was. His sex life—or lack thereof—was entangled with his crashed professional life. Repairing one didn't necessarily fix the other, but it would definitely be a step in the right direction.

He glanced up from his cocoa to see Todd looking around the bar and ignoring his coffee.

"Change your mind about the coffee?"

"Nah. I'm finding you a hot babe."

Sean sipped his cocoa, relishing the slow burn down his frozen throat. "Did it occur to you that I'm perfectly capable of finding my own 'hot babe'?"

"Yeah, right." Todd cursed. "There's no one even remotely your type in here."

"And what's my type?"

"Blonde lap dancers."

Sean laughed. That sounded about right. At least, that used to be right. He hadn't had a date in so long he didn't know what his type was anymore. The breathing type, probably.

"Yes! Got one."

Todd cocked his head at a bleached blonde woman giggling with two friends near a window. Blondie tossed her long hair over her shoulder and looked in Sean's direction. Her bright gaze took a leisurely ride down his body and then back up. Her lips parted, and her tongue moistened them with deliberation.

"There you go," Todd said with a nudge of his elbow into Sean's side. "I'll bet she's got a room upstairs. Go for it."

Two years ago Sean would have had the woman out of her ski bibs by now. Two years ago he didn't give a damn what or who he did. Two years ago he'd been a different person, and today the woman looking at him with an open invitation in her eyes didn't appeal to him at all.

"Not happening." He turned back to his cocoa.

Todd's head whipped around. "Are you insane?"

Sean had to wonder. He wanted to feel alive again. He *needed* to feel alive again. A naked woman beneath him could get him there. So why wasn't he jumping all over the blonde who might as well have *sure thing* tattooed on her forehead?

"Excuse me, sir."

Sean turned, and all thoughts of the blonde dissipated because he was staring into the most amazing eyes he'd ever seen. Their color, a dark, pure green, reminded him of a pine forest at dusk. Of woodland moss on the mountain's north face. Of the flannel sheets on his bed. Damn, but the cinnamon-haired beauty gazing back at him would look good tangled in those sheets.

What the hell? He'd just dismissed a slinky woman who no doubt would have guaranteed a night of steamy between-the-sheets play. And now this woman with uncontrolled shoulder-length hair and very little makeup on her pale, slightly rounded face—the polar opposite of the type of woman he used to date—piqued his interest. Piqued several things, as a matter of fact.

He swallowed tightly and willed his pulse to slow down. "Yeah?" Brilliant, Trenton. Just brilliant.

"Is the bartender around?" the woman asked in a sultry voice that sounded like early morning sin. "Oh, never mind. Here he comes." She gave Earl a smile Sean would kill to have aimed in his direction.

Earl slid a plate overflowing with fries and a hamburger in front of Sean. "Can I help you, miss?"

"Lemon drop martini, please."

Earl reached for a glass. "You got it. I'll take it to your table."

The woman thanked him and walked away, giving Sean a mouth-watering view of long legs and a curvaceous ass hugged by faded jeans. His pulse spiked higher than it had in a long, long time.

Todd, still drooling over the willowy blonde in the corner, seemed completely oblivious to her. "Sean. Buddy. Certain body parts are going to start falling off if you don't use them. You said you're ready."

"I am," Sean said, sounding idiotically short of breath and not nearly convincing enough. "I just have other things on my mind."

"Uh-huh. Chicken."

It was a trap. An appeal to Sean's competitive nature to prove Todd wrong. Funny, but knowing that didn't stop him from falling for it.

"I'm ready. Need proof?" Sean nodded at the martini woman, whose lush rear still swung in an enticing rhythm. "I'll ask her out."

Todd stared at him like he'd suggested they use butter to wax their skis. "Who are you, and where the hell is Sean?"

"What? She's hot."

Todd cast another glance at the woman as she skirted around several crowded tables and plopped into an empty booth next to the fire. "She's okay, but she's no lap dancer. Too tame for you."

Sean watched the woman wiggle into the seat and imagined her dancing—and more—in his lap.

Feeling a thrill of anticipation he hadn't experienced in years, he gave Earl a sharp nod. "I'll deliver the martini." The little fox by the fire didn't know it yet, but his dry streak was history.

Chapter Two

Robyn slumped against the booth's low backrest and stared at her cell phone. No signal. So much for following up on the panicked queries she'd made yesterday to potential replacement emcees.

With a low groan of frustration, she shrugged out of her jacket and waited for Karen to return from the gift shop. Their room wasn't ready, so they'd left their luggage at the front desk and settled in at the Moosehead Pub to kill time.

She'd have to wait until she could use the phone in her room, but hanging out in the bar wasn't much of a hardship. The fire was warm, the music soft but upbeat, and the aromas of burning wood and gourmet cuisine comforting.

Then there was the view. Forget the exquisite craftsmanship of the hand-carved furniture, railings and ceiling beams. Forget the massive stone fireplace that rose through the upper pub floors. The view that sent heat prickling over every inch of skin and nearly distracted her from her reunion troubles was that of the two gorgeous ski patrollers at the bar.

As a teen, she'd been forced to go on class ski trips, and rather than subject herself to the humiliation of riding single in a double-lift chair—because in snow gear she'd been bulked out even more—she'd hidden in the resort's dozens of cafés and fantasized about the patrollers as they brought injured skiers off the fifty-six runs, their confident competence a turn-on she couldn't describe. When they weren't helping someone, they flirted shamelessly with the guests, the employees, the skiers.

With everyone except her.

"Lemon drop martini?"

Shaken out of her past, she blinked her eyes back into focus and opened her mouth to thank the bartender. Only the man standing there with the sugar-rimmed glass in his hand wasn't the bartender. It was the patroller she'd spoken with briefly at the bar. The one with the inviting honey-gold eyes and the spiky brown hair streaked with blond. He was gazing down at her with a cocky grin that made her heart pound erratically in her chest.

She felt a sudden urge to ask him if he knew a game called hide-the-mitten.

"Uh, yes, the martini is mine." She cleared her throat to rid her voice of a sudden squeakiness. "Things around here have changed if the patrollers are doubling as cocktail waitresses."

"Well, we did draw the line at wearing skirts."

"Too bad. I'd liked to have seen that." At least, she'd liked to have seen if his legs were as toned and muscular as she suspected. She reached for her purse. "How much do I owe you?"

"It's on me." His grin turned sheepish—and even more attractive, if possible. "Literally. I spilled some on my jacket."

He glanced down at the wet spot on his sleeve, and she offered her napkin. "That'll get sticky."

The glass clinked as he set it on the table. "Sticky isn't always a bad thing."

His low, rich voice passed through her like a long-awaited caress. The man was her high school fantasy come true. Her two years with Damon had been emotionally draining. Maybe the time had come to recharge her batteries and take her mind off her troubles with a fun fling like Karen had suggested. So what if flings weren't in her nature? This trip was about change and discovering herself.

And about not looking like a moron in front of her former classmates.

She smiled up at him, wishing she'd put on makeup and done something with her hair instead of taking frump to a whole new level. "Care to join me?"

"Are you sure?" His hesitation intrigued her. He'd brought her the drink, surely as a come-on, but he suddenly seemed almost...nervous.

"No, but I'm feeling dangerous today."

"Works for me." The booth seat creaked as he sank down across from her. What would Karen say when she returned and found Robyn sitting with this tanned hunk? She'd be green with envy.

"Thanks for the drink."

"Any time." He held out his hand. "I'm Sean."

For a moment she stared at his long, well-shaped fingers, oddly uncertain. Something told her that once she touched this man there'd be no turning back, no flushing him from her mind even if he disappeared afterward.

Oh, for heaven's sake. Enough melodrama. This wasn't one of her teenaged daydreams where a handsome man had seen beyond her plain, pudgy face to her mind and fallen madly in love. This was reality, and she could flush this guy any time she wished.

She grasped his outstretched hand and tried to ignore the electricity that sparked at the contact. "Robyn."

His gaze jerked up from where their hands met, and as she pulled free, she knew the electric sensation had been mutual. "Are you here for the ski competition?"

Desperately needing a moment to recover from the tension that arced between them, she sipped her martini and shivered at the bittersweet explosion of citrus vodka on her tongue. "High school reunion, actually."

For some reason he looked pleased, and then he frowned. "A winter reunion?"

"All of the schools around here hold winter reunions. It's tradition."

"Now that you mention it, I think I've heard that. Isn't there some sort of charity tradition, too?" He peeled off his red patroller jacket, and she nearly drooled at how the tight-fitting thermal shirt beneath hugged his broad chest and the sharply defined muscles of his arms.

Gripping the stem of her glass a little tighter, she nodded. "Every class picks a charity at graduation and holds fund-raisers during their reunions."

And she'd been so eager to show off her success that she'd jumped all over the opportunity to put the fund-raiser together. *Idiot.*

He gave an approving nod, as well as a killer smile that made her erogenous zones sit up and take notice. Why couldn't she tear her eyes away from his lips? Probably because they looked firm, sensuous, perfect for kissing.

"What's your class charity?"

She took another sip of her chilled drink to counter the heat working its way through her veins. It didn't work. "Ski-Do. They fund ski trips for at-risk and underprivileged kids."

"I'm familiar with it. It's a great organization." He tipped his head, his gaze drifting down to her mouth, her throat, her breasts, and back up, taking so long she almost began to squirm. "What reunion is this for you? Five-year?"

She rolled her eyes, but secretly delighted in his charm. "I do believe my insincere flattery radar just went off."

He threw back his head and laughed. And what a nice laugh it was. She could listen to it all day. But not all night. At night there would be better things to do. Things her sex-starved body hadn't experienced in a long time. And no doubt Sean knew his way around a bedroom.

"I was serious. You can't be a day over twenty-five."

"It's my ten-year reunion, and I'm twenty-eight. Your turn."

A group of skiers clomped past the table in a ruckus of loud voices, and Sean nearly had to shout his answer. "My ten-year was a year ago." The obnoxious skiers moved on, and Sean lowered his voice. "So, how far did you have to come for your reunion?"

"From Chicago. I've lived there for six years. And you? Been in this area long?"

"I moved here almost two years ago from Montana." Twining his fingers together over his flat stomach, he sprawled back in the booth with a lazy grace that would have looked insolent on anyone else, but only appeared self-assured on him.

"So...you're a ski patroller-slash-cocktail waitress in the winter, but what do you do when the snow's gone?"

His amused one-sided grin created an adorable dimple on his right cheek.

"I pout for a week and then go to work for a private ambulance service as an emergency medical technician."

It was her turn to be pleased. No flashy jobs for this guy. Unlike Damon, Sean was perfect fling material. A ski fanatic who worked to support his snow habit. She could practically feel his strong hands, lightly dusted with tawny hair, slide over her sensitive skin, and heady anticipation like she hadn't felt in months—no, years—made her almost giddy.

She licked her lips, preparing to suggest they meet up later for dinner or drinks or...dessert, but a voice interrupted.

"I can't leave you alone for two minutes, can I?"

Karen had materialized out of nowhere, was standing by the table, one hand on her hip, the other hand clutching shopping bags. An appreciative smile curved her mouth as she gave Sean the once-over. Then a twice-over. Before things got out of hand, Robyn cleared her throat and scooted over to make room for her friend.

"Karen, Sean. Sean, Karen."

Karen's eyes flared. "Robyn, uh, where's the ladies' room?"

Robyn pointed to a recessed area on the far side of the bar, but the other woman shook her head. "This place is huge. I'll get lost. Can you show me?"

"Show you? Karen—"

Karen gave her a look that said "Do it or I'll kill you in your sleep". Robyn turned to Sean. "I'm sorry. My friend here has suddenly turned into an infant."

His mouth twisted wryly. "I have two sisters. I'm familiar with the female instinct to form herds for bathroom trips."

Robyn led the way to the bathroom, and once inside, she laid into Karen. "What is wrong with you? He's going to think we're nut cases!"

Karen peeked under the stall dividers. Apparently satisfied they were alone, she straightened and swung around. "Do you know who he is?"

"Yeah. A hunky ski patroller who is probably making a

getaway as we speak."

"You really don't know, do you?"

A sinking feeling tugged at Robyn's insides. "He's just a guy." Oh, please let him be *just* a guy.

Karen caught a glimpse of her sandy, wavy hair in the mirror and paused for an agonizing second to smooth a few strands. "He's just a guy who won an Olympic medal and has a gazillion product endorsements under his belt."

"That's ridiculous." Robyn sighed, relieved Karen had clearly mistaken Sean for someone else. Her plans for a steamy fling were still on. "Why would he be earning squat as a patroller? And how would you know anyway? You hate sports."

"But I love the Olympics." Karen took a deep breath, and the first stirrings of nausea churned in Robyn's belly. "I saw a story about him on TV. He won a medal—bronze or silver, I can't remember—and after that he pushed a bunch of cereal and lip balm. Always had the hottest model or movie star on his arm. Then, a month before he was supposed to ski at the next Olympics, he dropped out of the running." She paused. "Rob, he was the favorite for the gold in several events."

Stunned, Robyn propped a hip against the sink before she fell over. This could *not* be happening. "Why'd he drop out?"

Karen shrugged. "An injury, I think."

"Are you sure it's him?"

Her friend's nod snuffed out Robyn's last wisp of hope. "Positive. He looked familiar when I first saw him, but I knew for sure when you said his name." Karen gave her a sad smile. "If you're looking for an anonymous boy toy, he's definitely not it. You couldn't do worse if you tried."

Great. A fling with a guy like him wasn't worth the aggravation no matter how sexy he might be. In fact, a brief indulgence with Sean would be worse than what she'd had with Damon.

Flings simply didn't exist when reminders were thrown in your face every few weeks. Who knew when she might turn on the TV and see Sean in a commercial or as the subject of a news story? Or maybe he'd ski in a future Olympics and become the next media darling.

Bad enough having to listen to Damon on the radio and see him in his spot on Chicago's morning show, and on billboard and bus ads.

"So...what are you going to do?"

Robyn swallowed her disappointment like a lump of flavorless gum and reached for the door handle. "Well, I won't be playing hide-the-mitten with him, that's for sure."

Basking in the heat of the fire, Sean chewed on a soggy fry from the plate he'd retrieved while he waited for Robyn and her friend. Todd, who should have been heading to work, had joined the blonde sure thing, but by the looks of it, she'd turned into more of an iffy thing. For all Todd's big talk, he was the master of crash and burn.

Sean gulped his now lukewarm cocoa and cast a glance at the bathrooms. What was taking so long? The sooner he asked Robyn out, the sooner his nerves would settle down and the sooner he could stop worrying if he was still as good at hiding his jitters as he used to be.

He dragged a fry through a puddle of ketchup, and when he looked up again, his heart skipped a beat at the sight of Robyn walking toward him, her chunky-heeled leather boots clacking on the floor and adding an extra two inches to what was probably a five-foot-seven frame.

Damn, she fired him up, and he had no idea why. She was

shorter and had a fuller figure than he usually went for. Her hair was darker and more simply styled than he'd always liked. Everything about her was so opposite of the plastic, made-up dolls he'd wasted time on in the past that he might as well stop taking note of it.

Except that taking note of everything about Robyn was a hell of a lot of fun.

She slid into her seat, but Karen, who, with her long blonde mane and waif-like figure was the type of woman he used to go for, had stopped to munch pretzels from one of the bowls that lined the bar top.

"Everything okay in there?"

Robyn knocked back the last half of her martini. "Fine," she said when she finished.

Her tongue slipped out to lick the sugar from full, smooth lips that would tempt a saint, and his body tightened. Pathetic that the simple action could generate such a strong response, but at least he was feeling something other than indifference.

Clearing his throat, he glanced at his watch. He'd need to scoot if he wanted to feed Norbert and change for his appointment at the TV studio tonight, where he'd be meeting the man who held Sean's future in his hands. "So, Robyn, what are you doing later?"

She gave him a strange, sad smile as she ran a finger over the rim of her glass and sucked the sugar off her fingertip. His blood went south and throbbed violently in his groin.

Talk about pathetic.

"I was thinking about spending the evening in bed." Something intense flared in her eyes, and a soft blush swept over her cheeks as she dropped her gaze to her glass.

A ripple of excitement collided with a sudden stream of

anxiety. Now was the moment he should ask if she wanted company. Now. The line had always worked before.

So why did nothing come out of his mouth? Maybe because the deep-rooted stab of fear he'd been living with had only grown sharper since the disaster with Jenny, and as eager as he was to get physical with Robyn, he was also terrified.

The irony that he'd plummeted down sheer cliff faces at the summit of mountains accessible only by helicopter, but felt terror at the thought of hopping in the sack with a beautiful woman didn't escape his notice.

Unfortunately, she never gave him a chance to ask if she wanted company in her bed. "My flight did me in. I need to get to sleep early."

He wasn't sure if he should be insulted or relieved, but he was definitely confused. Had he misread her signals? Earlier, she'd seemed receptive to getting to know one another.

And to make matters worse, Todd was sauntering toward them like a used car salesman on a mission.

Fuck.

"Hey," he said to Robyn. "I'm Todd. Todd Davis." He dropped down beside her, and Sean nearly groaned. "Has my partner gotten around to asking you out yet?"

Grinding his teeth, Sean shot Todd a warning glare. "Don't you have to go to work?"

Robyn arched a brow. "Aren't you guys already at work?"

"We were off the clock fifteen minutes ago," Todd replied, reaching for one of Sean's fries.

Sean stabbed his hand with a fork.

"Ow!" Todd jerked his arm back and gave him a sullen look.

In the flickering firelight, Robyn's remarkable eyes glowed with amusement. "I'm glad I didn't ask for a bite."

31

The temperature of Sean's blood rose a few degrees. "*You* can have a bite anytime." A bite, a kiss, a lick...

And there was the sad smile again. "Well," she said, gathering her purse, "our room is probably ready. I need to go."

A twinge of panic twisted his gut. He couldn't lose her now, not the one woman who'd roused his interest for the first time in too long to think about. "Wait. Meet me for a drink tonight."

She shook her head, probably turned off by the desperation in his voice. "Sorry. Can't."

Todd casually leaned back in the booth and threw an arm over the back, blocking her. "Come on. Take pity on the guy. His dry spell has lasted longer than the Sahara's. Help him get the ball rolling again."

If Sean could have crawled into a hole and died, he would have. The heat in his face now had nothing to do with Robyn or the fire crackling nearby.

Robyn's lips quivered with the need to smile, and her husky voice dripped with laughter. "I'm sorry, but I'm not interested in rolling Sean's balls."

"Sean's ball," Todd corrected. "I said he's trying to get the *ball* rolling, not balls."

"You know," Sean said in the lightest tone he could manage, "I'm not sure I'm comfortable with this conversation about my balls."

"Or lack of them." Todd grinned. "Chicken. Ask her out."

"He did ask me out. I refused." She nudged Todd with her elbow. "Now, if you'll excuse me, I really need to go."

Sighing, Todd shoved to his feet and let her scoot out of the booth. Karen joined her, and with a "See you around," they were gone.

Sean admired Robyn's sexy, swinging retreat. After she

disappeared, he stood and socked Todd hard in the arm. "Thanks a lot, asshole."

"What?" Todd rubbed his shoulder. "I was trying to help. You weren't doing so hot on your own."

No argument there. "So I'm a little rusty. And you're still an asshole."

"Does she know who you are?"

"I don't think so."

Shaking his head, Todd moved toward the door. "Then you set your sights too high. I told you she's no lap dancer. She'll make you work too hard for it. Find a nice groupie who wants to put a notch in her bedpost. Or pick a cougar. Take baby steps, man. Baby steps."

"Jesus, Todd! I'm not learning how to walk." A couple of women at a nearby table who were probably cougars—bored divorcees who hung out at the resort to snag rich, high-society men or hard-bodied, young playthings—looked in their direction, and he lowered his voice. "I don't need a woman who wants to exchange bodily fluids but not names."

Christ. Where had *that* come from? Of course he wanted an easy lay with no strings attached and where names were optional. That's who he was. That's who he'd always been. Nothing had changed.

He ignored the niggling voice that told him everything had changed, and caught Todd staring at him with a "you are certifiable" look again.

"It's sex, Sean. Tab A into slot B. Humans have been doing it for thousands of years. It ain't rocket science. Find a lap dancer and get it over with."

Irritation at Todd's words and his own failure with Robyn fired Sean's blood, and he clenched his fists at his sides. More people stared now, but he was too angry to care. "Don't go there. You have no idea what I've been through. None."

That wasn't entirely true; Todd had been at his side during the worst times of his life, but his friend rarely acknowledged what had happened, was as uncomfortable with the subject as Sean was, and used humor to cope.

Todd hung his head and took a deep breath. When he looked up, his expression was uncharacteristically serious. "I know. But the longer you wait, the harder it's going to be." He smirked, back to his normal lecherous self. "Pun intended." He checked his watch. "I'm late. See you tomorrow."

He strode off and Sean returned to the booth, where he stared at his cold burger, no longer hungry. Todd was right. He'd blown the sex thing out of proportion. Tab A into slot B. How difficult was that?

He glanced at the blonde in the corner and at the divorcees downing margaritas as they scanned the room for victims. Not difficult at all. A nod and a wink would get him the blonde *and* a friend for the night.

But dammit, they did nothing for his tab A. He wanted Robyn. He had no idea why, but he did. And since this was the first woman he'd felt so strongly about in a long time, he was going to go for it, easy or not.

From what he'd seen, she wouldn't be easy. Funny, but somehow that thought thrilled him.

And made him question his sanity.

Robyn tried not to waddle as she stepped inside the empty elevator and pushed the button for the second floor. She and

Karen had eaten dinner in the lodge's elegant top-floor dining room, and Robyn had foolishly ordered dessert, a decadent white chocolate cheesecake with raspberry-brandy sauce. Ignoring her food guilt, because this was a vacation and she could afford to indulge a little, she was now ready to collapse into her soft, warm bed. A bed sadly empty of one sexy ski patroller.

Oh, but she could have had an amazing time with that guy. The man was made for flings. For intense, whirlwind dates, suggestive conversation, and wild, down-and-dirty, all-night sex. Moisture pooled between her thighs and her body temperature skyrocketed just thinking about it. She definitely didn't need a soak in the bubbling whirlpool spa, where Karen had gone while Robyn gulped down her dessert.

No, she'd follow up on the calls for an auction replacement she'd made from her room earlier, and then she'd get some much-needed rest. With any luck, one of her DJ friends from nearby Denver would come through for her on such short notice. Six days wasn't much time.

The elevator ground to a stop at the sixth-floor cafe, and the doors slid open. A man stood there, shock and disbelief playing on his pale face. Stunned herself, Robyn gaped.

It couldn't be.

It was.

"Damon," she gasped.

"Robyn." He stepped inside the elevator and enveloped her in a hug as if he were happy to see her, but his tense, rigid body said otherwise. "How are you?"

It was then that she noticed the tall, svelte blonde with him. Bewildered by his presence and his reluctant greeting, Robyn wrenched away. "Did you change your mind? Are you here for the auction?"

Please, please, say yes.

She hated herself for hoping he'd save the day, but desperation had shredded her pride.

His gaze flickered to the woman and back to Robyn. "I, uh...what are you doing here?"

"Why are *you* here?" she asked, angry and disappointed that, obviously, he hadn't come to fulfill his obligations. She jammed the second-floor button with her thumb, a little harder than necessary, and the doors whooshed shut. "You told me you weren't coming. Why'd you lie?"

Damon's distinguished face clouded with guilt, obscuring everything she'd ever found desirable. Gone was the attractive, confident charmer, and in his place was a tired show-off who tailgated on the highway and was a lousy tipper. How had she been so blind?

"I didn't lie," he growled.

"You told me you were canceling, but you're standing right here! How is that not a lie?"

Shame darkened his eyes, but only for a moment. "I never said I wasn't coming. Just that I had to cancel the emcee thing." He scrubbed his hand over his face. "This is damned inconvenient. We shouldn't even be having this conversation. The desk clerk assured me that our rooms were across the lodge from each other."

It was just like him to turn this into someone else's fault. He was famous for shifting the focus with indignant anger when he'd been the one who'd screwed up.

"I'm so sorry you had to go through the hassle of asking for distance between our rooms so I wouldn't find out you were here. But you know, I'm glad we ran into each other. Now I know what a snake you truly are."

She turned to the slinky blonde, who wore a petulant frown, as though she couldn't decide if she was uneasy or inconvenienced with the situation. "Good luck. You got yourself quite a guy. We'll compare notes someday."

He patted his shirt, probably looking for a pack of cigarettes. "Be careful, honey. You'll find yourself out of a job."

The elevator stopped on her floor, and a bitter laugh escaped her as she exited. "You wouldn't."

His hand slammed against the doorframe, holding the doors open. "Try me."

She wouldn't give him the pleasure. He always complained about her lack of spontaneity, so she'd show him some. "Go to hell. I quit."

Not quite believing she'd actually said that, she started down the hall. He told the woman to hold the elevator, and then his heavy footsteps pounded on the carpet behind her.

"Robyn, wait." When she didn't stop, he grabbed her elbow and jerked her to a halt. "Come on. Don't do this. I didn't mean it."

Shaking her head, she wrenched free of his grip. "I can't work with you anymore. It isn't good for either of us. We both know that. It was only a matter of time."

He knew. She saw it in his eyes. But she also saw his bruised pride and the fact that he wasn't about to lose face in front of the other woman, who now looked annoyed as she held the doors open. How utterly Damon.

"Are you sure this is what you want? You won't work for Mogul Media again."

"Excuse me?" She'd expected a sharp backlash, but not this. "You can't do that!"

"I'm a major stockholder. I can make it happen."

She lifted her chin. "I'll get a job with a competitor."

"You don't think I can arrange it so you'll never work in radio again? A few phone calls is all it would take."

The desperate gleam in his eyes told her more than his words did. This wasn't about saving face. He really didn't want her to quit. But why?

She glanced at the woman in the elevator. The leggy blonde could be a soap opera star or European royalty—both were just as likely in a place like this—and suddenly Damon's behavior made sense.

"Oh, my God," she breathed. "You want to keep me around until I can get you that interview with *Rolling Stone.*" For someone who craved fame and fortune but had found it only on a local level, national exposure would likely be the only way he'd feel like he belonged amongst real celebs.

Stunned by the realization, she staggered back a few steps. Had she been nothing more to him than an instrument to advance his career? Ice spread through her insides as every happy memory of their relationship came into question. Had he always been after something from her? No, not in the beginning. Not until he got the job with the TV station and she'd mentioned that her friend, Brad Hardy, had been hired at the popular music magazine.

"Please don't do this, Robyn. Don't back out on your promise."

"Like you did when you cancelled on the auction even though you'd planned to be here all along?" she shot back, and he didn't even have the decency to act remorseful.

Disgusted and unable to look at him for another second, she fled to her room, with Damon close on her heels. She reached into her pocket for her key, and her fingers closed around the cold metal—a nice change from impersonal plastic key cards—just as she reached the door.

"If you screw me over," he warned softly, "I'll crush you."

"Do your best. I won't go down without a fight."

That sounded tough, but her hand shook as she jabbed the key toward the old-fashioned door lock. She missed. And missed again. Damn it! Tears blurred her vision until she couldn't even see the doorknob anymore. She wasn't going to stand there like some pitiable loser while Damon and the blonde watched.

Determined to keep her dignity, she calmly shoved the key in her pocket and stalked down the hall toward the stairs without sparing either of them a glance. It was a small victory that her tears didn't fall in front of them, but the moment she rounded the corner she could no longer hold them back. Damon's lies and betrayal stung, but far more painful was the fact that on top of everything, she was now jobless. Her one consolation was that things couldn't get any worse.

Chapter Three

Things got worse.

Robyn sank down on the bench inside the spacious wooden phone booth and hung up the receiver. The dull beat of music from the Moosehead across the lobby pulsed inside her skull, aggravating the headache that was starting to throb.

She'd just learned from her mom that her parents' bakery would be providing the food for the reunion party on Thursday night and Robyn's help would be appreciated.

Helping wasn't a big deal. She loved working at the bakery. The big deal was that she'd been through this before. Her parents had catered several class functions and no matter how wonderful the food, it always earned Robyn torment.

"Robyn smells like the stinky cheese in the tarts."

"Robyn, if you didn't hang out at the bakery, you wouldn't be such a cow."

"Robyn eats all her parents' profits."

She wrapped her arms around her middle and threw her head back against the wall. Maybe she should save her classmates the trouble and tape the "kick me" sign between her shoulder blades right now.

Someone tapped on the window in the door. Startled, she jumped up and slipped out of the booth with a mumbled apology. What now? She didn't feel like returning to her room, and she'd already given up on whining to Karen, whom Robyn had found flirting with a guy in the Jacuzzi. Well, if Robyn couldn't get a little tonight, at least maybe her friend could.

The sounds of laughter and clinking glasses drew her attention to the bar. She wasn't one to drown her sorrows in alcohol, but at the moment, one or two—or ten—stiff drinks sounded like one hell of a plan.

She entered the fire-lit Moosehead and looked for a quiet, private table, but the place was packed. The only available seats were at the bar. The bar where she'd first seen Sean.

Great. She didn't need to be thinking about him, either. What she needed was something only the bartender could give her.

She positioned herself on a stool at the far end, grabbed a drink menu...and froze when she noticed the photo of Sean hanging on the wall next to the shelves of liquor. *Oh, my.* He wore a sleek, muscle-defining ski suit, his arm raised in victory as he slid across a finish line. She hadn't noticed the picture before, but boy, did she notice now.

He looked ecstatic, captivatingly alive in a way that transcended the stillness of the photo. Warm tingles whispered over her skin, and she had to drag her eyes away before she started fantasizing about things that could never be.

A platinum-haired bartender with a goatee slapped a napkin in front of her. "What can I get for you? This evening's special is a Screaming Orgasm."

Of course it was. She ordered one, figuring it would be the closest she'd get to the real thing tonight.

The bartender returned with her drink. She stirred the

vodka, Kahlua and Irish cream blend as all around her people laughed and toasted their day on the slopes. In the corners, couples snuggled, secretive smiles on their faces. Depressing. Utterly depressing. One of those smiling women could have been her, and one of those men with his arm around his date's shoulders could have been Sean.

Suppressing a sigh, she took a sip of her drink. Mmm, sweet and creamy and...

She nearly choked at the sight of Sean standing on the second level laughing with a woman who looked vaguely familiar. What was he still doing here? Not that she cared. But he didn't waste time, did he? His bedpost was probably so notched it looked like chainsaw art.

She took another sip of her drink. A large sip. Then she tried not to stare at Sean's smile as he propped one hip against the railing and spoke with the leggy woman, who kept touching him with not-so-subtle brushes and pats. A moment later she made her move with the most obvious of female signals announcing availability, the hair flip.

Nine-point-five for execution and presentation, a solid ten points for skankiness.

She had to give Sean credit, though. His body language, the way he drew away from the woman's ever more intimate touches, indicated he wasn't comfortable or interested. In fact, his gaze roamed the bar as though searching for something, and just as Robyn decided to move before he saw her, he did exactly that.

His eyes locked with hers, and a slow, one-sided smile tipped the corner of his made-for-sin mouth, stealing her breath and causing an unwelcome coil of carnal hunger to settle low in her belly. He straightened, his height and athletic build impressive in jeans and a black sweater. He spoke briefly with the woman and gestured to Robyn. Robyn stirred in her seat as the woman turned and gave her a weak smile. Why did she look so familiar?

Leaving the lady behind, Sean bounded down the stairs and crossed the floor, drawing every female eye in the establishment. The way he looked at Robyn, like she was the only woman on the planet, sent her pulse rate into orbit, and she had to put down her glass because her hand began to tremble.

God, she should *not* feel this way about a perfect stranger— especially not a perfect stranger who embodied everything she hated about ski culture and who had the potential to bask in a large spot of limelight.

"Hi," he said in a low, intimate tone that brought to mind images of fireside snuggling and lazy morning lovemaking. Before she could utter a word, he bent and brushed his warm lips over her cheek. "Baby, where have you been?"

Confused, her skin tingling where his lips had caressed it, she glanced upstairs to where the woman watched with narrowed eyes. Ah. He needed help. And she did owe him for the martini...

What the heck.

Smiling wickedly, she slipped her hands under his sweater, caught two fingers in the belt loops on either side of his waist, and tugged him forward between her knees. His breath hitched in surprise and a brown eyebrow shot up, but he didn't complain.

"Where have I been?" she purred. "Looking for you, of course."

A second eyebrow joined the first. The man had very expressive eyebrows. "Seriously?"

"Um, no. Aren't we playing ditch-the-stalker?"

His rumbling laughter vibrated his hips against her knees, and she had to stifle a gasp at the shock of desire that sizzled through her. "Any game that puts me between your legs is one I want to play."

He moved closer until her thighs hugged his slim hips. Heat spread upward, through her pelvis, her chest, until even her breath scorched her throat. Then, before she could protest, his mouth came down on hers, softly, just barely, but enough to hint at the pleasure that mouth could give.

Disappointment and relief collided when he drew back and cast a furtive glance upstairs. The woman was gone. "Thanks. This is the third time I've had to dodge her talons."

He made no move to extract himself from between her legs now that his stalker had been thwarted, and in fact, his hands rested intimately on her legs, his thumbs lightly stroking the sensitive flesh of her inner thighs. Even through the barrier of her jeans, his touch made her pulse leap, her skin burn.

"I could get used to being in this position," he murmured, and shifted his weight, creating a tantalizing pressure against the seam of her jeans with the fly of his.

Her throat went as dry as sawdust. She could get used to him being there, too.

No, she couldn't. Wouldn't.

With regret, she let go of him and cleared her parched throat. "What did you tell her?"

Her blatant change of subject seemed to amuse him, and he chuckled as he pulled up a bar stool. "That you're my very jealous girlfriend."

He had the jealous part right. She'd never been secure enough in any relationship to keep the green monster at bay. She did, however, have a sense of humor, so she smiled archly and reached for her glass. "And what would you have done if I hadn't played along?" she teased.

"I have no idea. Gigi's a man-seeking missile. She'd have reacquired her target in no time."

"Gigi. Gigi Anderson?"

He shrugged a shoulder. "Beats me what her current last name is. She's a cougar. A divorcee looking for a man," he added when she looked at him in confusion. "She's been on the prowl for husband number three or four for a couple of months."

Robyn gulped down her drink and signaled the bartender for another. Gigi had been one of her cruelest tormenters in high school, and though Robyn had thought she was prepared to see people like Gigi again, her old fears and insecurities had just breached the wall she'd believed to be impenetrable. Her anxiety made no sense, not now that she had done so well for herself. But Gigi had been ultra-vicious, ultra-popular, and— oh, God, no, was walking toward them.

Old habits died hard, and Robyn instinctively sought an escape route. The bathroom was too far away. The main door was behind Gigi. The chimneys were full of fire.

She was trapped.

And if that wasn't enough, she looked as frayed as she felt after a day of flying. She hated that Sean had to see her in this state, but truly, if there was one person for whom she'd wanted to look her best, it was Gigi.

And Heidi. And Felicia. And about two hundred and ninety-seven others from her graduating class of three hundred.

"I'm sorry to interrupt." Gigi stopped next to Robyn. "But I know I've seen you before. Have we met?"

Robyn's throat closed up. Gigi, wearing a form-fitting designer ski suit that was obviously for show only, given that her hair and makeup appeared too perfect for her to have been skiing, was as beautiful and glamorous as ever, and suddenly Robyn felt like the homely troll people laughed at when they'd tripped her in the halls. Abruptly, Sean's strong hand settled over hers, and his energy trickled through her skin all the way to her spine, which stiffened. Somehow, she found her voice.

"We went to high school together. I'm Robyn Montgomery."

Gigi scowled, her eyes going blank as she tried to remember. "You're coordinating the auction, right?" Robyn nodded, and Gigi shook her head. "I'm sorry. I don't seem to remember—"

She broke off, her face splotched with crimson. For a moment she just stared, her mouth working silently for words. Finally, a smile trembled over what had to be collagen-enhanced lips.

"Oh. Robyn. How nice to see you looking so...good. I'd say you haven't changed a bit, but..."

And how did one respond to that? Robyn had dreamed of this moment for years, had planned down to the word what she would say and how she'd say it. Now none of the spiteful words came. Instead, she managed a polite, "Nice to see you, too."

Gigi dropped her gaze to Robyn and Sean's joined hands. The other woman's smile still trembled, and were her hands doing the same? Gigi was definitely flustered, something that should have brought Robyn more than a little satisfaction, but strangely, didn't.

"I-I suppose I'd better go. Will I see you at the reunion get-together on Thursday?"

"Definitely."

"Great." Gigi waggled her fingers at Sean in a goodbye gesture. "Ta-ta! Tell Toddy hello."

Sean smirked. "Will do. He'd love to see you again."

Gigi perked up and sauntered off, and Robyn slumped in relief. As soon as Gigi was out of earshot, Sean laughed.

"Todd'll be dodging her for weeks." He squeezed Robyn's hand. "What was that about? I could have skied on the tension between you two."

"It was nothing." She took a large sip of the drink the bartender had just left and then groaned as a thought popped into her head. "You told her I was your girlfriend!"

"Yeah, so?"

"So, I hope you're up to performing some boyfriend duties."

His honey-colored eyes darkened to a smooth, liquid caramel that made her want to dive in. "Like what?" he asked, his voice deep and smoky and seductive.

Unable to resist the draw of his voice, she angled her body closer to his, delighted that his breath came a little faster. "Like being my date at the party Gigi mentioned."

She braced for a refusal. Reunions weren't fun for anyone, especially someone else's. But instead of a horrified look and a ready excuse, Sean only grinned.

"If it means I can convince women like Gigi that you're the hottest thing around, then yeah, I'm up for it."

An unexpected thrill coursed through her at the compliment. "What do you mean? She's gorgeous!"

"Did you get a good look? She's been ridden hard and put away wet." His gaze slid down Robyn's body and back up in a very blatant, very appreciative appraisal that made her blood simmer. "She's got nothing on you."

The guy was smooth, she'd give him that. "You need to get your vision checked, but I'm not going to argue. Thank you. For the compliment and for being my reunion date."

He rubbed his thumb over the suddenly hypersensitive skin of her wrist. "Negotiations aren't over yet."

"No?"

"No."

He signaled the bartender and ordered a local microbrew. When he finished, he brought her hand to his mouth and pressed a lingering kiss into her palm, creating fluttery sensations in her belly. She couldn't help but wonder what a kiss to a more intimate part of her body would do to her.

"I'll go to the reunion if you'll have dinner with me tomorrow."

How had this gone from a simple drink in the bar to dating a guy she'd already decided wasn't acceptable even for a fling? She didn't want to go to dinner. She didn't want to take him to the reunion even though the reactions she'd get would be priceless. She wanted nothing to do with him. She didn't need another Damon.

But she did need a date, and no doubt Gigi was right now phoning the old gang to report the fact that Robyn the Troll had caught a hottie. There was no way she could go to the reunion without Sean now.

"Fine. But this is for show only. Nothing is going to happen between us. Nothing. Got it?"

He smiled. "Sure."

"You're humoring me."

The bartender brought his bottle of beer, and he took a swig. "Yep."

"Why?"

"Because," he said in a low, husky voice, "I want to kiss you again. And I think you want it, too." He reached out and touched the backs of his fingers to her cheek, and it took all she had not to close her eyes and lean into his light caress. "And if that leads to something else, then, well, we'll see."

She had no idea what to say because God help her, she wanted to kiss him and more just like he said, so she closed her shaky hands around her glass and drained it.

And here, she'd thought things couldn't possibly get worse.

✳ ✳ ✳

Sean watched Robyn stir the contents of her third Screaming Orgasm and wondered why she'd shut down like an overloaded chair lift. She'd agreed to move to a more comfortable seat, and now she just sat there, her expression contemplative and distant.

They were sitting in an intimate upstairs corner near a snow-flocked window, in a curved booth softly lit by flickering candles on the table and crystal sconces on the walls. He lounged back, one leg propped up, his knee touching hers. She, on the other hand, sat stiffly, legs together, spine straight, much like she had when Gigi approached earlier.

And what was that all about? Had they been rivals for boys in high school? His sisters had had similar rivalries, so the theory made sense. What didn't make sense was why she was still so on edge.

"Is everything okay?"

She raised her gaze from her drink and let out a weary sigh. "I know who you are."

"As in...?" His fingers itched to play with the glossy fox-red strands of hair that brushed her shoulders as she shook her head, but he settled for peeling the label off his beer bottle.

"As in, was it a bronze or silver medal?"

"Ah, that." Disappointed that she was aware of his identity, his gaze drifted to the far wall, where an enlarged photo of him accepting his Olympic medal hung in a place of prominence. The photo was one of many the resort owners had scattered about after they'd hired him as a patroller.

You don't mind if we use the fact that we have an Olympian in our employ for promotion, right? the owners had asked—two weeks after they'd hung the pictures.

"Silver. Missed gold by two-hundredths of a second." Baffled by her almost imperceptible nod and devastated expression, he shifted a little closer to her. "I don't get it. Why doesn't that make you want to jump my bones?"

A burst of laughter brightened her eyes and chased away his concern. "How did they get the medal over your swollen head?"

He smiled and shook his head. "No, I mean, it's just—" He took a deep breath and tried to figure out how to dig himself and his swollen head out of this. "Usually that's the only reason women want me." And in the past, he'd played the sports-hero card freely and often.

Her gaze roved unhurriedly over him, and when her eyes met his, the heat in them made his breath hitch. "Oh, I doubt that."

Her four softly spoken words sent his heart rate into overdrive. "Is the athlete thing a problem for you?"

The heat in her eyes chilled. "Only if I want to like you."

"I'm not following." But he had to admit, it was an interesting twist. Here was a woman who didn't want him *because* of who he was. His opinion of her ramped up several notches.

Outside, the wind picked up, rattling the windows. Robyn studied the snow slapping against the glass, and just as he
50

began to wonder if she would speak, she turned to him.

"I've been in and out of a relationship that was all about appearances and public life. I hated it. Hated being the nameless girl on the arm of the star. I don't want to do that again." She drew little circles on the table with a French manicured nail as she spoke. "I know I'll only be here a couple of weeks, but that just makes things worse. I don't want to go home and then hear about you on the news or see you in commercials."

That he understood. Three years ago he'd dated a supermodel, and after a nasty breakup, her digitally enhanced face had mocked him from magazines, television, billboards...she'd been everywhere.

"Then I have good news," he said. "I don't ski competitively anymore, and no one has asked me to push a product in more than a year."

He saw no point in telling her about the sports-announcer gig since it might be a one-time thing. He'd met with his new boss this evening at the network affiliate's local TV studio, and although the guy seemed sure Sean would be hired on a permanent basis, he got a sleazy vibe from the man and didn't trust a word.

Either she was amazingly intuitive, or his tone had betrayed his lingering bitterness, because her voice softened. "Why don't you ski competitively anymore?"

He tipped his beer bottle to his lips, more to give himself a moment than because he was thirsty. After several swallows, his throat didn't feel so tight. "Took a bad fall. Broke my leg and a couple of ribs."

"During practice?"

"Yeah." No, but only his family and Todd knew the truth. He took her hand in his and caressed her silky smooth palm with his fingers. "My turn. You know all about me, but I don't know anything but your name."

She shrugged and looked down at his hand as though trying to decide whether or not to allow his touch. "Not much to tell. I grew up here, went to college in New York, and until an hour ago I was the music director at a Chicago radio station."

"An hour ago? What happened?"

"I got into it with my boss." She slipped him a sideways glance. "What are you doing here, anyway? You couldn't have been trapped by Gigi for *that* long."

He gave a theatrical shudder that wasn't entirely feigned. "God, no. I had a meeting in town earlier. I came back to drop off some supplies for the patrol office. When I tried to leave, I got mobbed by Gigi and a bunch of her minions who wanted autographs—"

He broke off and gave himself a mental kick in the ass for mentioning the autograph thing. Nothing like reminding her of the very reason she didn't want to jump his bones.

Robyn rolled her bottom lip between her teeth, and he pulled a ragged breath into his lungs. He wanted those lips on his so badly he could do nothing but stare at her mouth until she finally heaved a deep sigh.

"I'm sorry," she said, "but it's almost midnight and I'm beat, and these drinks have gone to my head. I think I'll call it a night."

"I'll pay our tabs and walk you to your room."

"Nice try, but no thanks."

"The tabs or the room?"

"Both. I can walk by myself, and I can pay for my own drinks."

"I know you're capable of walking by yourself, but I want to see where your room is so I can show up unexpectedly." He scooted out of the booth and dug in his back pocket for his wallet. "And I'm going to pay for the drinks because I want to be responsible for your screaming orgasms."

She laughed, a sweet sound gave him a rush of pleasure. "Everyone knows today's women are responsible for their own screaming orgasms."

Now *there* was an erotic image that would have him sweating in frustration tonight. "You also saved me from Gigi," he pointed out.

"I saved you from Gigi as payment for the martini earlier."

He winked. "Guess you'll just have to owe me again, huh?"

She stood, shaking her head, but she smiled as she spoke. "You're a pain in the butt, you know that?"

"It's one of my many talents."

"I'm afraid to ask about the others."

He bent close, so close he could feel stray wisps of her hair brush his cheek. "I could show you." Yeah, the things he would show her...

She gave him an exasperated huff, and he laughed as he grabbed her hand and led her down the spiral staircase to the crowded main floor, where he paid the tab. As he waited at the bar for his change, he spotted his new network boss at a nearby table. He nodded in greeting, and then he and Robyn slipped out of the Moose and into a horde of people fresh in from night skiing, their jackets and hats dusted with snow. He placed a protective hand over the small of her back and guided her through mob, and it felt so good to touch her that he left his hand there as they climbed the stairs to the second floor. Her room was only a couple of doors down, to his acute disappointment.

"Well, this is it." She pulled a key from her jeans' pocket.

He waited while she opened the door and flicked on the light. After tossing her key onto the TV stand, she leaned against the doorframe and watched him, head tilted to one side, hair tucked behind one ear.

"Look." She sounded so tired that he wanted to wrap her up in his arms and tuck her into bed. Preferably a bed with him in it. "I'm sorry if I've been grumpy. I've had a really bad day. I'd love to have dinner with you tomorrow, and I'm more grateful than you can imagine that you're willing to go to my reunion with me."

"There's nothing to be grateful for. I'm doing it for purely selfish reasons."

"And what would those be?"

"Well," he said, bracing one hand on the wall next to her head and leaning in, "if we're going to play boyfriend-girlfriend, we need to practice." He dipped his head, letting his lips brush the tip of her delicate ear, and her light vanilla-berry fragrance nearly made him dizzy with wanting. "We have to be convincing."

She turned, her lips mere centimeters away from his, her brow furrowed. "Sean—"

He covered her mouth with his, smothering whatever she'd been about to say. She went still. Heart racing, he seized the advantage, flicking his tongue over her smooth lips until a tremor rippled through her and she opened up to him in a soft, warm meeting that tasted of rich coffee liquor and sweet Irish cream.

Oh, man, she could kiss. He cupped her cheek with his free hand, and she melted against him, her hands sliding up his chest in a way that made his body clench and his skin burn.

The sound of laughter at the other end of the hall brought

him to his senses, and he drew back, shifted his body to shield her from the newcomers' view. She blinked up at him with passion-glazed eyes. A surge of male pride shot through him because, oh, yeah, he hadn't lost his touch.

His gaze cut to the open doorway. Mere footsteps away, the mattress beckoned. It may have been forever since he'd shared a bed with a woman, but he wasn't so rusty that he didn't remember how to get a woman into one. Slanting his mouth over her lips, he took Robyn's mouth again in a hungry kiss that she encouraged with an arm hooked around his neck.

A shock of desire zinged through him, making every point of skin-to-skin contact with her spark. He brushed his hand along her cheek and into her hair, finally, *finally*, threading his fingers through the glossy strands. A low moan from deep in her throat urged him on, and he pinned her against the wall with his body, shuddering when her firm breasts pressed into his chest.

Her hands dropped, and he prepared for her to shove him away, but instead she reached under his sweater and skated her palms over his abdomen, his pecs, his back...nearly everything she could reach. And then, oh, sweet hell, her stomach muscles contracted against his hard arousal, and his already simmering senses ignited.

It had been so long since he'd been with a woman like this. He knew he should back off, take it slow, but he was like a starving man who'd found food just in time. Taking too much would be a mistake, but his self-control was gone.

He couldn't get enough of her wet, wild taste, her exotic scent, her ample curves that filled his hand perfectly. He rubbed his thumb over the faint outline of her nipple as it strained against her sweater, but he wanted more, wanted to lave her breast with his tongue as he thrust inside her.

Shifting even closer, he wedged his thigh between hers. She arched against him and whimpered, the most welcome sound he'd ever heard. If he could just ease her through the door, kiss her as he guided her toward the bed...

The bed. A sudden wave of anxiety doused his heated thoughts. What if she found him as repulsive as Jenny had? He wasn't prepared to deal with that yet. Not tonight. Not after a long day and a nerve-wracking meeting with his new boss.

With a gulp of much-needed oxygen, he drew away again, this time breaking contact completely with a step back.

"Robyn," he said thickly, hoping she'd buy his excuse for backing off, "we'd better stop before Karen shows up and gets an eyeful."

She let out a long, shaky breath before calmly tucking her hair behind her ear again. "What makes you think I would have let you do anything that would give her an eyeful?"

He reached out to trace his finger along the line of her jaw, and frustration shot through him at the feel of her silky skin. "My irresistible charm?" She crossed her arms over her chest and tapped her foot on the floor sternly, but the corners of her lips were turned up in amusement. "Can't blame a guy for hoping."

"Well, ski-boy, you can hope all you want. I'm going to bed." She slipped inside the room like a slinky cat. "Alone." With a smirk, she shut the door.

He stood there for a moment, wondering how far he'd have gotten if he'd made some tried-and-true moves on her, but ultimately it didn't matter because he wasn't sure if an attack of nerves would keep him from being able to follow through.

How was he supposed to seduce her when he was afraid he'd choke at the last minute?

Cursing, he headed downstairs, where the night-skiers had

dispersed. As he cleared the last step, someone called his name. He turned to see his new network boss standing near the lobby fireplace. Sean extended his hand.

"Mr. Slade. Hello again."

"Please, call me Damon."

"Sure, Damon." Sean dropped the other man's hand and resisted the urge to wipe his palm on his jeans. "Enjoying your stay?"

Damon nodded. "As a matter of fact, I am. Would you care to join me for a drink?"

"Thanks, but no. I need to get home—"

Damon grasped Sean's elbow. "I'd like to speak with you for a moment. I'm sure you don't mind."

Sean did mind, but this was his boss, the man who could make him or break him, and he agreed. He tried not to think about the fact that two years ago, no one made him do anything he didn't want to do.

They walked toward the Moose, and as they entered the bar, a flurry of activity brought Sean to a stop. Two patrollers jogged across the lobby toward the lodge's front doors. One, a six-year veteran named Mitch, halted in front of him.

"A guy just fell from a lift. Wiped out three skiers on the ground. One is in cardiac arrest, and another has a pole impalement. We could use you."

"You got it." All patrollers had first responder training, but only a handful were certified EMTs like Sean, so his help could be useful. "What's the ETA of the victims?"

Mitch checked his beeper. "Two minutes."

"I'll be right there."

Mitch took off, and Sean turned to Damon. "I gotta dash."

Damon clapped a hand on his shoulder. "Give me one

minute. You have two."

Damn. The guy was slick. "What is it?"

"It's about Robyn."

Sean frowned. Surely Damon hadn't said what Sean thought he'd heard. "Who?"

"The woman you were just with. You forgot her name already?"

Hackles and temper rising, Sean struggled to keep his voice even. "I'm surprised you know her."

"I know her," Damon said in a tone that made clear exactly how well he knew her, and Sean bristled even more, which was strange, since he'd never been the jealous type. "And I need a favor. If you can keep her out of my way for the next couple of weeks, I'd be grateful."

Favor? Not even close. The man had issued an order. "You lost me. Why would I need to keep her away from you?"

"Robyn and I have a...history." Damon leaned a little closer and said conspiratorially, "We were supposed to be here together, and now I'm here with another woman. She could make life miserable for me and my date. A woman scorned and all that. You know how it is."

Yeah, Sean knew exactly how it was. He'd been in similar situations before, but that was a long time ago, and even then he hadn't been proud of his behavior. Damon seemed to be gloating—at Robyn's expense, something that made Sean's blood boil.

"I don't know if she told you," Damon continued, "but she lost her job, and I'm sort of responsible. I feel bad. So I'll tell you what. I'll make sure she has a position with Mogul Media, *and* I'll do my best to see that you get a permanent announcer job if you'll humor me and keep her busy until I have time to make it up to her."

Sean had a feeling there was more to Damon's generosity than he was letting on. If Damon felt bad for what had happened to Robyn, Sean would eat his ski goggles. Still, there was something desperate about the man, something that almost made Sean feel sorry for him. He reminded Sean of competitive skiers who had been at the top of their games, who had been good guys, great sportsmen, but who were past their primes and were struggling to make a comeback.

And who were bitter because it wasn't happening.

"Yo! Trenton!"

Mitch's shout and beckoning wave from the front doors lit a fire under him, and he turned back to Damon. "I have to go."

He stepped away, but once more Damon grabbed his arm. "Well?"

Sean gave a sharp jerk of the head. "I'll keep Robyn busy if it'll mean she gets to keep her job. Good enough?"

Damon's greasy grin creeped Sean out. "Great. I look forward to working with you. Oh, and let's keep this between us."

Sean nodded and trotted off, unease curling in his gut as he wondered what he'd just gotten himself into.

Chapter Four

Warmth enveloped Robyn's body as Sean's hands roved over the prickling flesh of her arms, her back, her legs. Her breasts crushed against his bare chest, the crisp hair tickling her nipples. She shifted her weight so his thick thigh pressed between hers, making her moan, wanting more.

God, she wanted him, especially when he whispered her name into her hair and told her how sexy she was. How hot. Then his minty breath tickled her cheek as his lips kissed a hot path from her ear to her mouth.

"Mmm, Sean." Stretching, she reached over his shoulder to caress the sculpted muscles of his back, but a shock of cold air on her arms froze her movement and jolted her into unwelcome consciousness.

Confusion fogged her brain. A dream. She'd been dreaming. Sean's hands weren't on her body. Her naked chest wasn't rubbing against his. His lips weren't kissing hers...but why then did she smell mint?

Her eyelids flew open, and through the fuzzy haze that no amount of blinking would banish, she saw Sean's golden brown eyes only inches from hers.

"You sleep like a rock."

"Omigod!" she croaked, sitting up as he straightened but remained standing beside her bed. "What are you—? How did you—?" Had she moaned his name out loud? Embarrassment stung her cheeks.

Slinging a cocky grin at her, he dangled a key between his fingers. "Karen thought you needed a wake-up call."

What Karen needed was a whack with a ski pole. Robyn should never have told her about the kiss she and Sean had shared last night. Still flustered, she tugged the blanket up around her neck, even though her flannel pajamas more than covered everything. "Wake-up calls are usually, uh, calls."

He gestured to the table near the window, where a tray laden with fruit, yogurt, waffles and bacon sat next to a carafe of what she hoped was coffee. "The food wouldn't fit through the phone lines."

"I can't believe you brought me breakfast." She swung her feet out of bed to the cold hardwood floor and ran a hand through what was probably a rat's nest of hair. "And I can't believe Karen just *gave* you the key to our room. You could be an ax murderer or something."

"Yeah, I get that a lot. You know, people thinking I'm a blade-wielding psycho."

Laughing, she stood and gave him a once-over. Oh, he was fine in his ski patrol jacket, black ski pants and ski boots. "Shouldn't you be out rescuing people?"

"I am. I'm rescuing you."

"From what?"

"This dismal room." Eyes gleaming with mischief, he reached out, grasped her waist and pulled her to him.

The thick material of her pajamas was no defense against his cold jacket. Goosebumps shivered over her skin, but the steamy glint in his eyes chased away the chill. Her body, still primed for him after the erotic dream, responded independently of her brain, pressing against him as if trying to relive the fantasy.

Then he kissed her.

It wasn't much of a kiss, barely more than a peck, but when he released her and stepped back, she stood there swaying like a teenage groupie who had just seen her first rock star. She desperately needed to get a grip on her hormones.

Clearing her throat, she gathered her wits and glanced at the food that must be part of his rescue technique. "Your job description isn't very clear, is it?"

His killer smile had her traitorous heart tripping all over itself. "You need to get out in the sunshine."

She peeked through her second-story window that was blocked by deep snow save for the one-inch space at the top. One more light snowfall, and even that small crack would be gone. It wasn't unusual for the snow to reach the fourth, and even fifth floors in the winter, and guests would often use the windows as coolers, sticking their bottles of drinks into the snow during their stay. "It's not sunny."

"It is at the summit." He checked his watch and slapped the key down on the dresser. "I'll see you outside, right?"

She rolled her eyes. "Yeah, yeah. Give me an hour."

What he gave her was another cocky grin. "You are really hot in the morning." With a wink, he was gone.

Legs suddenly weak and rubbery, she sank down on a chair. Sean's fun, uplifting energy amazed her. He clearly loved life and didn't seem to let anything bother him. He was the polar opposite of her. She worried about everything and could rarely let herself just...go.

Even her dreams had been full of angst. At least, they had been until Sean invaded them.

But now it was back to reality. The reality where she was going to get back on skis for the first time in years and where she didn't have an emcee for the auction. Even worse, she still had no job.

She had enough money saved to make the rent and car payments for a couple of months, but she did need work—and fast.

Hopefully Damon would calm down and not follow through with his threat to bar her from Mogul Media's holdings. They owned more North American radio and television stations than any other corporation, and if she wanted a job, they were the company to work for.

She hated that she still felt like she needed Damon for something, especially after what he'd done to her last night, but she was so far down in the dumps right now that she didn't know how to dig herself out.

Sighing, she plucked a slice of crispy bacon off the giant plate of food and nibbled on it while she checked her voicemail near the window, where her cell phone received a faint signal. Four messages. Two sorry-but-I-can't-do-the-auctions and two sorry-we-don't-have-any-openings-at-this-stations.

Had Damon already blackballed her? She wanted to scream, to pound on every single door at the lodge until she found him, and give him a piece of her mind. And maybe a piece of her fist in his face. That, at least, would give her a measure of satisfaction. Damon loved his surgically sculpted nose, and he had a talent for keeping it brown. Was Sean like that? She'd bet her last dollar that he didn't bother with schmoozing and brown nosing.

This was a guy who had gone from public figure to

anonymous, underpaid rescuer and appeared to be content. How refreshing. How noble. And how damned seductive when being seduced was the last thing she needed.

She tucked her legs beneath her and reached for a melon wedge as the memory of his mouth on hers last night turned over again and again in her head. No question, the man could kiss. He'd melted her very bones with his lips, his touch. And his assurance that he wouldn't be stepping foot into the spotlight again as a professional athlete had darned near brought her over to the dark side.

She was ready for a fling that wouldn't involve her heart, and Sean *did* say he was done with being famous.

But could she handle the women who threw themselves at him? The...what had he called them? Cougars? And what about the groupies? Surely there were women who would sell their souls to bed an Olympic medalist. Could she deal with that even for a brief affair?

It was all so complicated. She wanted him, but did she want the risks involved with taking him for a lover? She glanced at her cell phone, still flashing the message icon on the screen.

God, her life was messed up right now, her world upside down and nothing certain. And for someone who needed structure and schedules and security, nothing could be worse. Not knowing if she'd ever get another job or an auction emcee or even if she should hazard a fling with Sean left her feeling lost and vulnerable for the first time in years. Since the last time she'd returned home, actually.

And now here she was, preparing to immerse herself in the shallow winter sports culture she'd happily left behind years ago.

Turning to the open closet, she glared at the new ski outfit she'd purchased at the Downhiller Shoppe before dinner last night. Well, she'd promised to ski with Karen, and if she couldn't keep any other promises today, she'd at least keep that one. She'd spend a few hours on the slopes before diving back into her pool of despair. After that, she didn't know what to do.

"Look at me, Sean! Look at me!"

Sean grinned at the six-year-old skiing past at a snail's pace. The boy had only yesterday mastered the rope tow, and though Sean couldn't convince him to discontinue the "fall down" method of stopping, he had to admit the kid had a great attitude.

Sean gave him a thumbs-up and then waved to the Tiny Tots instructor, whom Sean sometimes got talked into helping. Not that he minded. Teaching kids to love the snow as much as he did was an opportunity he never passed up—and it was the reason he'd known about Ski-Do, the charity Robyn's class sponsored. He'd been their spokesman during his competition days.

"Sean Trenton? Is that really you?"

A twenty-ish man wearing a jester-style knit cap slid toward him with a big, goofy grin on his face and funky square sunglasses covering his eyes, even though the sun had yet to peek through the low cloud deck.

"Sweet! It *is* you. Can I get your autograph?" The guy gestured at Sean's jacket. "Ski patrol? Bummer. Nothin' like going from Olympic medal to that, huh?"

"Yeah, helping people is a major step down."

The guy nodded, oblivious to Sean's sarcasm. "No doubt." He took off a glove and fumbled around in his pocket before producing a pen. "I don't have paper, but you can sign my lift ticket."

"Lucky me." Sean scrawled his name on the ticket and handed the pen back.

The autograph hound thanked Sean and slid off, shouting to his buddies that he'd gotten an Olympic medalist's signature. Definitely Sean's cue to get out of there before he got swarmed by more autograph seekers who felt sorry for him.

But not sorry enough to not want his mark on something.

He jammed his poles into the snow to shove off, but stopped at the sound of his name—this time spoken by the one person he didn't mind finding him. Robyn. And she looked amazing in a cream jacket and ski pants, and a green headband, all of which would look even better in a pile beside his bed.

"I see you still have quite the fan base," she said with a fragile smile. Even though he understood it, he cursed her issue with fame and fortune, and as people began to look in his direction thanks to the loud-mouthed autograph seeker, he scrambled for damage control.

"Nah. That's a rarity. No one remembers me."

A big lie. With the ski competition and snowboard championships taking place in a few days, fans and groupies, skiers and non-skiers from all over the world, had taken over the resort. He'd been swarmed—and propositioned—several times during the last week. There had been a time when he'd have welcomed the attention and offers, but now he only wanted to escape.

Quickly, before anyone could catch him, he grasped Robyn by the elbow and eased her toward the nearest lift. "I saw Karen head up the hill a few minutes ago. She said she'd be skiing Thunder Run until you catch up with her. Wanna share a chair?"

"Where's your partner? Don't you have to go up with him?"

"Nope. He's waiting for me in the warming house at the top of Demon's Dive."

Heaving a theatrical sigh, she said, "I suppose I could bring myself to share a seat with you. You did bring me breakfast, after all."

As they moved forward in the lift line, he leaned close, letting his lips graze her cold-reddened cheek. "Breakfast in bed. Don't forget the 'in bed' part."

He certainly wouldn't. She'd looked so sweet as she slept curled into a flannel ball, her fiery hair fanned out over the pillow, her mouth curved in a gentle smile. He wouldn't mind waking up to that every morning, minus the pajamas.

And when she'd moaned in her sleep, flicked her tongue over her lips, he'd wanted so badly to kiss her awake, to make her moan for him instead of some stupid dream. He'd settled for a kiss on her cheek, a poor substitute.

She looked like she wanted to say something, but their turn at the ticket scanner came up, and they scooted into position for the lift. A chair swooped in behind them, and then they were swinging into the air and up above the crowd. Robyn's eyes sparkled as they climbed.

"I didn't realize how much I've missed this," she breathed.

"It never gets old, does it?"

She didn't answer. She didn't need to. The way she took in the view, hanging far over the chair's side railing, her gaze intense, said it all. Brushing a stray snowflake from the tip of her nose with one hand, she pointed into the distance with the other. "Why is that pine decorated with underwear?"

"That's the bootie tree." At her uncomprehending

expression, he elaborated. "Have sex with a stranger, collect their underwear, and toss 'em off the lift at the tree the next morning." He peered down. "Looks like a lot of people got lucky last night."

Her naughty smile made the blood rush hotly through his veins. "What if your partner doesn't wear underwear? What do you throw then?"

"Trying to tell me something?" Images of Robyn's bare body beneath her snowsuit flooded his head, and he shoved them away before his brain short-circuited.

"You have a one-track mind."

He brushed a strand of hair from her cheek and tucked it under her fleece headband. "I'm a guy. We all have one-track minds."

"Good point."

They continued up, and the temperature dropped sharply when they entered the cloud deck. Swirling mist surrounded them, growing so thick that the chairs in front and behind disappeared. Beneath them, the ground melted away in an ocean of gray.

Robyn blew out a long breath. "This is freaky. Like we're floating all alone."

"Alone is good."

"I'm not so sure about that."

"Mmm." He wriggled closer so their hips touched. "Why not?"

"Because I know exactly what I want, which, FYI, isn't you—until we're alone together." His pulse quickened as she turned her face up, her mouth so temptingly close. "And then I forget why I don't want you," she finished on a whisper.

Her lips parted and her tongue slipped out to moisten them

in a motion that was so unintentionally erotic that his chest constricted and his cock stirred. Had he ever wanted to kiss a woman so badly?

Knowing the answer and unable to wait any longer, he leaned forward, covered her mouth with his. Her lips yielded to the gentle nudge of his tongue, which tingled with the taste of her cinnamon gloss, so sweet and spicy, like the woman who wore it. A sigh that was a boost to his ego escaped her as she reached around to cup the back of his head and pull him closer.

As if he needed encouragement to crush his body to hers.

Arousal rippled through his veins, making him want more than what he could get on a ski lift above the timberline, especially when her hand slid down his arm to his waist, and then lower, where it brushed over his now straining erection and settled on his thigh. His fingers ached to touch her, and he tugged off a glove from the hand not holding his poles and slipped it under her jacket and sweater. The soft, bare skin there quivered at his touch.

Robyn moaned, arching against him and stroking his tongue with hers, deepening their kiss and turning it into something hungry and urgent. Plunging into the hot depths of her mouth, he smoothed his hand up her ribs until he found the lace edge of her bra.

This was crazy, feeling her up in a chair lift, but he didn't care, and apparently, she didn't either, because she shifted to give him better access. A low growl of approval rumbled up from deep in his chest as he brushed his thumb over the plump lower swell of her breast. A delicate shudder wracked her body, a purely feminine response that called out to the male in him to make it happen again.

Heat flared inside him, a slow burn of sensation that

threatened to grow out of control with every passing second. Her fingers squeezed his thigh, inches from where he needed her to be. Silently, he willed her to slide her hand up, to stroke him until the world around them ceased to exist.

"You can do some wonderful things with your mouth," she murmured against his lips.

Smiling, he dragged his mouth away, which was a good thing, since they had started to break out of the clouds. "Oh, I haven't even begun to do wonderful things with it yet."

She took a sharp intake of breath, and her cheeks, already flushed from the cold, flamed red. "Stop that."

"Stop what?"

"Stop making me forget that I don't want anything to do with you."

"No way, because I want everything to do with you."

Her chin came up, and she watched him for a long moment. "Why me? You can't tell me you don't have groupies and bobcats falling all over you."

He tugged his glove back on and flexed his fingers to warm them. "Cougars. And I gave that up a long time ago." He noted her pursed lips. "You don't believe me."

"Would you?"

"No," he admitted. "I've been around the sports world too long. When a guy says he's done with groupies, he means he's done until the next one flashes some cleavage."

"So how do I know you aren't just waiting for the next one?"

"I pursued you, not the other way around, remember?"

"I suppose..." She trailed off, a moment's pause before continuing quickly, as if she hoped to catch him off guard. "But what if I'd come on to you in the bar?"

"I'd do what I always do. I'd suddenly remember I was late

for an important meeting."

Liar. Had she jumped into his lap right there in the crowded room, he'd not have complained.

She slanted him a guarded look still edged with doubt, but at least she didn't call him on it.

Their chair climbed above the fog into clear air, leaving the deck of popcorn clouds below. The undiluted sun beat down on hundreds of miles of craggy mountain peaks as they pierced the layer of clouds stacked against them.

He never tired of the view, never lost that feeling of awe, but today the gorgeous woman beside him made the scenery pale in comparison. Her eyes, bright with wonder, took in the magnificent landscape, and her lips, parted slightly, glistened with his kiss. Nothing had ever been so beautiful.

Unfortunately, her run was approaching, and he'd have to let her go.

"How does six o'clock sound?"

She turned, blinking at him in confusion. "What?"

"You're having dinner with me. Remember? How about if I pick you up at six?"

"Oh. Right. That should work. I'm going to visit my parents, but I'll be back in time. Want to meet at Après Ski?"

"Sounds good."

The lift line leveled out and eased across the ski-run ramp. She slipped out of the chair and slid to the right with a wave, giving him a temporary, but tantalizing, view of her backside squeezed into tight ski pants. Talk about scenery. He winced and adjusted his aching arousal. Talk about uncomfortable. He really needed to get her into bed.

Gritting his teeth, he threw back his head and studied the morning sky. Six o'clock was a lifetime away. But if he could just hold on they'd have several hours together, time, perhaps, to get her over her celebrities-are-off-limits deal.

And time for him to conquer his own issues. Which he would. He always had. An athlete could only function properly if he faced his fears head-on. Not that he was an athlete any longer, but some lessons stuck with a person for life.

He had a helluva to-do list. And Robyn was at the top of it.

✳ ✳ ✳

Robyn hit the slope tentatively, her skills so rusty she was amazed she was still standing upright. More practiced skiers flew past, and she imagined them laughing at her as the taunts of the past echoed in her brain. God, why had she allowed Karen to talk her into this?

Because she needed a friend with her on this trip, that was why. Still, as her unsteady legs carried her down the run, she wondered if bringing Karen had been worth it. She tried to relax, tried to welcome the cold wind in her face as a remedy for the heat simmering in her veins thanks to Sean. But it didn't work. Heat still simmered, and tension still made her muscles clench. At least he wasn't here to witness her clumsy attempts at skiing.

A couple of women passed her in a spray of snow, their sleek suits a blur of color that screamed "look at me!" Karen had tried to talk Robyn into buying something similar, but she'd wanted to blend in with the slope and hopefully become invisible. So far, so good.

Yes, her paranoia and fear was ridiculous, but she hadn't confronted all the monsters of her past, something she'd hoped to do at the reunion. Conquering the slopes was a whole other monster.

By the time she reached the bottom, she was drenched in nervous sweat and her leg muscles screamed with exhaustion, but her childhood skills had started to return, and she'd dredged up a little more confidence.

She caught up with Karen near the lift, where she was flirting with the goth-guy she'd been hanging all over in the hot tub the night before.

"Rob, hey." Karen waved. "This is Freak."

Robyn nodded at the mega-pierced man. Karen's taste in men had always been a mystery. "Hi. I'm Robyn."

"Nice to meet you." Freak leaned toward Karen, whispered something that made her blush, and then slid away on his snowboard. "Later."

"Isn't he cute?" Karen said with a sigh.

"Sure. In that way crocodiles are cute."

Karen giggled, something she did only when a man was involved somehow. "So...tell me how it went this morning."

"You mean when I woke up to some strange guy in the room because *you* gave him a key?"

"Exactly." Karen grinned, utterly pleased with herself. "Don't tell me you wasted the opportunity."

"What opportunity? To get him into bed?"

"Of course. Didn't you say you were torn? I figured I'd help you along."

Robyn groaned inwardly. After Karen returned to the room last night, they'd sat up and talked until three a.m., and she'd admitted just how tempted she was to jump Sean's bones now that she knew she wouldn't be seeing his face on TV.

"Thanks." Robyn didn't bother hiding her sarcasm as Karen steered her toward the chair lift. "But I'm still torn."

"The groupie thing?"

"Mostly. He said he was over that…"

"But you don't believe him."

She shrugged. "I don't know. I believed everything Damon told me, and look what happened."

"Personally, I don't think it's a big deal even if Sean is lying. It's not like you two are getting married or anything. But the fact that he's chasing you and not the other way around sort of proves he's telling the truth, don't you think?"

"That's the argument of the day."

"Then just do it. Do *him*."

"We'll see."

Karen rolled her eyes and Robyn sighed. She was ready for a casual fling. She was. Of course, she had to fight her very nature over that one. She took life—and relationships—seriously. No matter how hard she'd tried, she simply could not separate her emotions from anything.

Which was part of what frightened her about Sean. Had he been a pretty face in a shallow shell, a casual relationship might have been possible—she'd done it before. But he appeared to be so much more, someone she could fall for if she wasn't careful. Could they keep things fun and low-key?

Maybe she was concerned over nothing. Tonight she'd get to know him better, and maybe, just maybe, he'd shatter the illusion he presented of being perfect. He'd reveal his flaws and she could have her fling because her emotions wouldn't get in the way.

So it was settled. She'd give him some rope and let him hang himself.

Bells tinkled as Robyn opened the door to her mom's bakery, Hausfreunde. Translated into English, Friends of the House suited the quaint shop that regularly burst at the seams with people her mother considered friends, not customers. Today was no exception. The tables were full and a line of customers waited at the counter for service. Regulars chatted amongst themselves, and new customers admired the collection of German-crafted cuckoo clocks and pictures of grand mountain chalets on the walls.

Robyn wove her way through the crowd, mouth watering at the mingled aromas of savory baked breads and sweet pastries. They were the smells of comfort and happiness and childhood. The bakery had been the one place where she found solace from the cruel world outside, and today she sought solace from all her confused thoughts about Sean.

"My baby girl!" Gretchen Montgomery's faint German accent rang out as she hurried from the kitchen to engulf Robyn in a huge hug. Before she could catch her breath, her mother dragged her into the kitchen and hugged her again. "You look good, honey! A little thin, I think, but we can fix that."

Robyn sighed. Her mother thought everyone could use an extra ten pounds. "Where's dad?"

"He'll be here any minute with your brothers. They're all going to help with your reunion menu."

The reunion. Robyn's stomach lurched. Sure, she had a date now, but the auction was still a lost cause if someone didn't answer her plea for help soon. "I heard you donated a gift certificate to the auction."

"Several local businesses donated something for a door prize."

"Sis!"

Twenty-three-year-old Joe, her youngest brother, dropped a

box of supplies and sauntered toward her like a nearly grown puppy still not comfortable in its body. His long arms swallowed her in a bear hug and before he let go, her other brother and father joined in the group hug.

"Guys," she said with a laugh, "I can't breathe."

They all pulled away and Greg playfully tugged on a lock of her hair. "If you can talk, you can breathe."

She punched him in the arm. "I should've remembered that, since you used to sit on me until I couldn't do either."

"Hit Joe, too. He helped."

He'd had to. Her younger brothers had both grown taller than her by the time she reached fourteen, but she'd outweighed them until well after high school.

"We're glad you made it," her dad said with so much enthusiasm no one would have guessed her family had been in Chicago for Christmas only weeks ago.

Greg tore open a case of yeast. "We weren't sure if you could get time off from work."

"Oh, no worries there." She had more time off now than she knew what to do with.

Taking a deep, soothing breath of the fragrant air, Robyn watched a young baker pull some dark, round loaves of bread out of the ancient German masonry oven her parents had shipped from Europe. The wood-fired heat baked the most delicious crusty artisan breads she'd ever tasted.

"Well," her mother said, "are you ready to get your hands dirty?"

More than ready. Nothing relaxed her more than working with dough, so a couple of hours spent elbow deep in flour sounded like heaven.

And it was heaven, until two hours later, after mixing

several batches of various dough, preparing three linzer tortes and shaping loaves of nine-grain, ciabatta and Parmesan levain breads, she was ready to get away from her brothers' good-natured ribbing and face dinner with Sean.

She was not, however, prepared to face him now. Not while covered with flour and smelling like a prune tart. So it figured he'd walk into Hausfreunde as she was walking out.

"Hi." He held the door so she could step out onto the salted sidewalk that ran in front of several blocks of chic, upscale boutiques and gourmet bistros.

People swarmed the streets, hands full of shopping bags and drinks in plastic cups. An all-year-long party atmosphere had always dominated the city, which, during the height of the tourist season, operated almost twenty-four-seven. Music blared from posh bars that catered to the rich and famous and attracted travelers from all over the world.

Sean let the door swing shut, and there in the chilly afternoon air with said tourists skirting around them, he ran his finger along her cheekbone in a slow motion that did funny things to her insides. "This is a nice look on you."

Flour coated his fingertip and she winced. "It's the new thing, you know. All-natural cosmetics."

He laughed that great laugh of his. "What are you doing?"

"I'm heading back to the lodge so I can meet you."

"In that case," he said, "let me walk you to your car."

She shook her head, wanting to escape as quickly as possible before he caught a whiff of her. "It's okay. My rental is just across the street."

"Indulge me."

If only he knew how tempted she was to indulge in whatever he wanted. "So you want me to satisfy your Boy Scout fantasy?"

"I want you to satisfy all my fantasies."

This time his words didn't do funny little things to her insides; they did serious big things to her insides. With a smile that made her knees weak, he grasped her hand and walked with her across the freshly plowed street to her four-wheel-drive wagon. She dug her keys out of her purse, but he took them from her and opened the driver side door.

She watched him through narrowed eyes. "Are you always such a gentleman, or is this an act?"

He closed the gap between them, and his warm hand came up to cup her cheek. His touch scorched her, left her breathless. "What does your gut tell you?"

"It tells me to run," she whispered, trying to look away, but his broad shoulders blocked everything but him.

His finger brushed along her jaw and down her throat to the top of her cowl-neck sweater, and her blood heated, pooled in all the places it mattered. "Why?"

"Because it might not be an act."

He leaned fractionally closer, and she bumped up against the rear door. He followed, his body touching but not pressing. "And that's a bad thing?"

If he only knew. She could deal with come-ons and blatant attempts to get her into bed if she recognized the efforts for what they were. She could prepare her heart and mind for shallow relationships. And yes, Sean obviously wanted to get physical, but unlike many men of her past, he didn't look at her like she was good for only one thing. Sean seemed genuinely interested in *her*, not just her body.

And that was the danger. As a teen she'd been so desperate for acceptance that she'd fallen for every nice thing people said, only to be crushed later when the nice thing proved to be a joke. Growing up fat and homely had taught her some harsh lessons. Lessons reinforced by her work in the media world, where sincerity and depth were façades, and she had no defense against the real thing.

"It can be a bad thing." She sucked in an icy breath as he placed his hands on the roof of the car, one on each side of her, caging her in, bringing to mind thoughts of being beneath him like this. "When I'm trying to resist you."

"Why would you want to do that?" He nuzzled her ear and her mind turned to mush.

Why? She suddenly had no idea. She couldn't think when his lips were kissing a trail from her ear to her mouth. Then his mouth met hers and the battle was lost. Surrender had never felt so good.

A needy moan escaped her as she welcomed the taste of him, welcomed the insatiable hunger that consumed her at the first flick of his tongue against hers. His kiss was hot and deep and wet, and so skillful that she couldn't help but wonder about—and anticipate—his other talents.

She slid her hands under his jacket, partly for warmth, partly so she could feel the muscles of his back leap under her palms. Sean shifted, his hard thigh parting her legs as he pressed closer, and oh, it felt nice to have him there between her legs again.

His hands still on the roof of the car, he surrounded her with his taut body and his blistering warmth and his light, clean scent. She moved her palms up to his shoulder blades and pulled him closer so her belly encountered the heavy bulge at his groin. A ragged breath shuddered from his lungs.

"You feel good," he murmured against her lips, "and you taste incredible."

The rough edge to his voice fueled the fire she'd been fighting since she met him, and she dropped her hands to his firm, denim-covered rear, pulling him closer. A pleasant tightening sensation settled deep between her legs where his thigh pushed against her, and thank God they were standing outside in the cold on a busy street, or else she might have been tempted to pursue some of those fantasy ideas of his.

Busy street...her parents' shop...this had to stop. Now. "Sean. I-I have to go."

He brushed his lips over hers. "So soon?"

"I'm freezing," she lied, because she was burning up inside, but he didn't need to know that. "And I'm getting wet."

One corner of his mouth curved into a bad boy smile. "A guy likes to hear that."

Puzzled, she frowned, and then she got it. "Jerk," she said, laughing. "You wish!" She pushed him away and patted the wet spots on the back of her jeans while pointedly looking at the car. "Water. Snow. My pants are wet."

Thankfully, he let it go, but the twinkle in his eyes told her he could have ridden that horse all day long. "I'll see you tonight." He gave her a peck on the cheek and then jogged across the street, his stride effortless and smooth, something she could watch for hours.

With a sigh, she settled into the vehicle and started the engine. She just kept getting in deeper and deeper, and it was only a matter of time before she drowned.

Chapter Five

"Which one? The blue, or the green?"

Karen looked up from the fashion magazine she was flipping through to study the sweaters Robyn held up for her opinion. "Green flatters you the most. But the blue is tighter. Makes your boobs look even bigger. Sean'll like that." She gave a small, secret smile. "Not that it matters, since I'm sure you won't be wearing it for long."

"Nothing is going to happen." Nothing more than what had already happened, anyway. Not until she was sure she could keep emotions out of their relationship.

Karen snorted and rolled her eyes, so certain of her prediction that she apparently didn't feel the need to respond.

Robyn laughed and stuck out her tongue. "You're just jealous."

"That you're having dinner with the most gorgeous guy I've ever seen, even if he isn't my type? Nah." She nodded in approval when Robyn returned the green sweater to the closet. "Does your bra and underwear match?"

"What did I just say? Nothing. Is. Going. To. Happen."

"So that's a yes?"

With a huff, Robyn tugged off the sweater she'd been wearing when she ran into Sean earlier. "Yes."

Karen tossed the magazine aside and stretched out on her bed, propping her head in one hand. "So tell me again how 'nothing happened' outside your parents' bakery."

"Sean ambushed me. I was caught off guard." Knowing that excuse sounded as lame to her friend as it did to her own ears, Robyn grinnėd. "And it was nice."

"Nice? It was *nice*?"

"Okay, it was beyond nice." Her thoughts turned inward as she replayed the kiss they'd shared against the car. Even now, her breasts tightened and her skin tingled. "Karen, I turned into a hot puddle of goo."

Karen's eyes got a dreamy look in them. "I'll bet that man is as talented in the bedroom as he is on the slopes."

A strange tremor of both feverish desire and icy distress ran through Robyn as she pulled the navy angora sweater over her head. No doubt Sean could steam up a bedroom, but the reason he could—the hordes of women who had no doubt given him the practice—left her cold when it should have made her happy.

It was exactly the kind of flaw she was looking for.

She couldn't be with Sean because of who he was, and she'd best get used to that.

Desperately needing to change the subject, she dug her hairbrush out of her makeup bag and plopped down on the bed next to Karen. "Are you seeing Freak tonight?"

"Yep. He'll be here in a few minutes to pick me up. We're doing a little night-skiing. He's going to teach me to snowboard." Karen waggled her eyebrows playfully. "And me? I'll readily admit to wearing a matching bra and panties."

"Which translates to no bra and panties?"

"You know me way too well."

Robyn dragged the brush through her hair. Her friend had a great thing going with Freak, and Robyn had to confess to a twinge of jealousy. She'd come to the resort hoping to find an average, non-celebrity guy she could enjoy without worry, a fun fling she'd remember fondly and without regret ten years later.

Instead, she was more worried than ever, and sure regret was only a matter of time.

She checked her makeup in the bathroom mirror before grabbing her jacket off the back of the chair near the door. "I'm out of here. I need to go before the crowds get too big outside." She shoved her room key in her jeans' pocket and opened the door. "I'll see you later."

"Have a good time," Karen called out as Robyn stepped into the hall. "I won't expect you back until tomorrow."

"I told you—"

"Yeah, yeah. Nothing is going to happen." Karen shooed her away. "Get out of here. Go!"

Robyn shut the door and stood there for a moment, leaning against it. She felt a little overwhelmed, a little wide-eyed with a sensation similar to terror...but not quite. Her body hummed with nervous energy, and with something else that wasn't welcome—arousal. Just thinking about Sean got her hot and bothered. She had no idea what that meant.

And she wasn't sure she wanted to know.

Robyn shouldered her way through the night-skiers in the lobby, repeating to herself that this was nothing more than dinner and fun. She wouldn't get attached or have *too* much fun.

When she stepped outside the lodge where it should have been dark, bright lights nearly blinded her. Blinking, she peered through the glittering curtain of fat snowflakes at a television camera crew, a reporter and six members of the Italian, Norwegian and US ski teams who'd arrived for Saturday's competition.

The athletes stood in the trampled snow, laughing, joking, checking out the women in the crowd, their smug grins and self-assuredness guaranteeing they wouldn't sleep alone tonight. She could so easily picture Sean doing the same not long ago, and her stomach churned.

Pushing her way through the throng, she moved away from the suffocating activity—and ran into Damon.

"Hello, sweetheart," he said, cheery and amiable, as if he hadn't threatened to crush her less than twenty-four hours ago.

"Don't call me that," she gritted out, and then, unable to resist baiting him, she nodded toward the cameras. "Hoping to get in front of them?"

"Supervising."

Puzzled, she glanced at the network symbols on the cameras. Several weeks ago, Damon had mentioned he'd taken a large role in the production of the Mogul Media's winter sports interests. His being here now made sense, and it hit her; he'd known he'd be here *months* ago when she asked him to emcee the auction. He'd acted as though he'd be going out of his way to help her out, but he had planned to be here for the ski competition all along. That *bastard*. She wanted to punch him, but instead, she smiled. Maybe she could twist the situation to her advantage.

"You know, this could be a great opportunity for you." She gestured to the camera crew. "You could emcee the charity auction and get footage of you doing it."

And what a huge boost for Ski-Do to have their cause featured on TV.

"Sorry, sweets. I have an important party to attend after the ski competition."

She stared in disbelief, though this was, after all, Damon, so nothing should come as a surprise. "So your schmoozing parties are more important than keeping your promise to raise money for underprivileged kids."

"Maybe I can arrange for someone else to give you a hand." He looked down at her with a wolfish smile she used to think was cute. "If you help me out."

Unbelievable. "If I give Brad Hardy a call for that interview, you mean." She shook her head. "I'd rather emcee the auction myself." Besides, she didn't trust him not to go back on his word the moment she made the arrangements.

His laughter stabbed at her like a knife. "You? You couldn't speak in front of a crowd if all you had to do is lip synch." He crowded close and lowered his voice. "Let me help you. I really do feel bad about last night."

Of all the crazy things, she actually believed he did feel bad. But she also knew he was ruthless when he wanted something. Damon was a businessman to the core. "If you want to make it up to me, you'll emcee the auction, and *then* I'll contact Brad. You know my word is good."

"No deal." He shouted a command at one of his crew and turned a cold eye on her. "Why are you harassing me, anyway? Don't you have someplace you need to be?"

Oh, God. Sean! She glanced at her watch. Ten minutes late. She took off without another word and trekked across packed snow through the brightly lit ski village adjacent to the lodge. Most of the glass-front shops were still open, and she had to step around crowds of window shoppers and bar-hoppers as she hurried to Après Ski, a split-level log and stone pub done up like an earthy, miniature mountain ski lodge.

Sean waited on the porch, his shoulder propped casually against the wooden railing, arms crossed, sharp eyes scanning the hordes of pedestrians. He smiled when he saw her and she should have known he wouldn't be angry. Did anything rattle the guy?

"Hi," he shouted over the music that blasted from inside the bar when someone opened the door to enter.

"I'm so sorry," she said as she climbed the steps to meet him. "I ran into my ex-boss and got stuck dealing with him and his stupid camera crew." She stomped snow off her boots. "Have I mentioned how much I detest the media circus? How much I detest *him*?"

Something flashed in Sean's eyes, gone too quickly for her to tell what it was. "But your career is in radio, right?"

"Yes, but I mostly work behind the scenes."

"Do you like your job?"

An interesting question, and one she wasn't sure how to answer. She used to love what she did, but now...not so much. "My job has its plusses. But that doesn't mean I have to like the people in TV and radio."

"True." He slung his arm around her shoulders and steered her toward the staff parking lot at the end of the village. "You hungry?"

"Starving."

He bent his head and dragged his lips over her ear that was still ringing with the echoes of music from the bar. "So am I."

Her breath caught and words left her, which was just as well since he pulled away to dig keys from his pocket. He stopped beneath a bright streetlamp on the passenger side of a huge, beat-up old Land Rover. A light dusting of snow coated the green paint, but not enough to hide the dents and deep scratches. She had to admit that she was more than a little surprised that he wasn't driving something new and expensive.

He opened the door, and she climbed inside. The interior was clean but just as abused as the outside. "How long have you had this thing?" she asked when he bounded into the driver's seat.

"Since I was eighteen. It ain't pretty, but it can carry a lot of ski gear and EMT equipment, and it can't be beat in the snow. I grew out of my sports car phase a couple of years ago." He inserted the key into the ignition and the engine rumbled to life. He gave her a sideways glance as he drove out of the lot. "What do you drive? A sexy two-seater, I'd guess."

She shook her head. "I grew up in the land of SUVs, so that's what I've got."

Her SUV was a luxury model that wouldn't know what to do in deep snow, but the vehicle was a symbol of how hard she'd worked to get where she was, to where she could afford such extravagance, and she loved it even if it was more of a dainty show horse than a practical beast of burden.

"My kind of girl." He reached over and took her hand. "But then, I knew that."

She decided she'd keep her mouth shut about the truth of her SUV.

Sean drove like a maniac on the main roads, but once they turned off onto a snowy backwoods mountain trail that would have made her SUV balk like a high-strung stallion, he eased the vehicle along until they arrived at a small log home.

"Wow." She climbed out of the truck and wished it weren't dark outside so she could better see the surrounding forest and frozen stream that snaked around the floodlight-lit house. "Is this yours?"

He took her hand and led her onto the porch. "Yep. It's not much, but it works for me."

Not much? The place was wonderful. Rugged, welcoming, with just the right touch of masculine elegance. The moment they walked inside, heat from the wood stove in one corner of the great room enveloped her, and a fluffy gray tabby trotted across the hardwood floor to greet her with a bump against her shin.

Sean scooped the cat up and gave it a playful rub between the ears before putting it down on the knotty pine-framed couch, which matched the rustic, outdoorsy décor.

"You don't strike me as a cat person," she said, when the purring feline ran back to weave between Sean's legs.

"I wasn't until I got Norbert." He bent to remove his boots and she did the same before her idle hands ended up on his perfect rear.

"Norbert?"

"From the *Angry Beavers*." He looked at her like she was a complete moron when she stared at him in incomprehension. "Cartoon."

"Ah." He watched cartoons and *she* was the moron? "So why'd you get a cat if you didn't like them?"

He peeled off his jacket and took hers to hang on the coat hooks beside the door. "He's a stray. I can't get rid of the fleabag."

"Liar." Not only was the cat clean, fat and happy, there was way too much affection in Sean's voice to believe a word he said. "Spill."

He shrugged, and a splash of red stained his cheeks. "No biggie. I was on EMT duty and saw some idiot toss a kitten out of a car window. My partner and I stopped, patched him up and drove him to the vet."

"And?"

He rolled his eyes. "I paid for his care and got stuck with him."

"Didn't you get in trouble for having an animal in the ambulance?"

"Oh, yeah." He tossed a toy mouse across the floor and Norbert chased it, batting it around the room. "But it was worth it, I guess. He's a cool little guy."

Norbert took his mouse up the stairs and she turned to Sean. "So, do I get a tour?"

"What you see is what you get. The kitchen is over there." He gestured to a modest, modern kitchen on the left. "The stairs lead to the loft, my bedroom. Bathroom is up there, too. Like I said, it's not much..."

"It's great." She glanced at the sparse furnishings, all neatly arranged. "And tidy."

Another blush crept into Sean's cheeks, giving him a boyishly appealing look. How odd that he'd been so confident before, but now, on his own turf, he seemed less so.

"I wanted to impress you. It's normally a disaster. And the décor?" He paused and scrubbed his hand over his face. "I can't believe I'm telling you this. I only bought the cabin because it came furnished. I suck at decorating."

She doubted he sucked at anything, but she let that one go. She sniffed the air, and her mouth watered at the hearty aroma of beef and onions. "Something smells wonderful."

"It's just stew in a slow cooker. Make yourself comfortable. I'll grab some wine."

While she waited for him, she wandered around the living

room, admiring his various medals and trophies and plaques that sat on shelves and hung on walls next to the decorative antique snowshoes, skis and wildlife oil paintings. True-life adventure novels and videos labeled with various dates and worldwide locations filled the bookcase near the TV.

"What are these?" she asked, when he returned with two glasses of red wine.

He sat on the couch and threw his feet up on the coffee table, crossing them at the ankles. "Training videos, some competitions." He shrugged. "Nothing exciting."

"Can I watch one?"

"If you want."

As she sipped her wine, she ran her finger over the titles and stopped at one labeled "Swiss Alps Helo-hell". She raised a questioning eyebrow.

"Go ahead. You'll get a good chuckle."

He used the remote to turn on the TV and VCR, and after she inserted the video, she joined him on the couch, careful to keep a few inches between them. Sean hooked his arm around her waist, dragged her close and leaned back in a lazy, casual sprawl.

"I won't bite," he murmured against her cheek.

She rolled her eyes. "I know, I know. Unless I want you to. I've heard that line before."

"It's no line. I wouldn't ruin your skin with bite marks. Licks are another matter..."

Robyn had to chomp down on a lustful moan. The man would be the death of any sane ideas she had to keep things tame.

On the TV screen, static merged into blue sky. A helicopter swooped into the frame, sunlight glinting off its surface. It slowed until it stopped, hovering at the summit of a snow-capped mountain. The aircraft's side door opened, and a man clad in a royal blue snowsuit and helmet leapt from the opening into the empty air.

"Is that you?" Robyn asked, sounding as breathless as she suddenly felt.

"Yup."

Sean hit the pristine snow in a puff of powder between two large boulders. Pointing his ski tips downward, he attacked the slope. And no question, *attacked* was the only way to describe what he did to the mountain.

She had been a skier almost since birth, and she'd been good, had shown a lot of potential—until she gained weight and turned into a klutz. At least, she thought she'd been good and had potential. Until now, as she witnessed the magic of Sean's freeskiing.

Literally on the edge of her seat, she held her wine glass so tight she had to remind herself to loosen her grip else shatter the glass. The man sitting so casually next to her, his hand gently massaging her tense neck, was crazy. Absolutely insane.

On the screen, he tore up the slope with relaxed grace and unwavering balance as he slammed left and zigged right, going airborne over jagged rocks. The spectacle was both breathtaking and terrifying. The power of his moves, the strength he must possess in his legs and torso...

"I love that," he said so softly, so intimately, that he could have been speaking of a lover. "Being alone out there. There was a camera crew, but they were at a distance. It's so quiet, just me and the mountain. Nothing even comes close to that feeling."

A familiar ache tugged at her, the ache that came with a hole in one's life. Had she ever been so passionate about anything? Had she ever known the fulfillment of doing something for which she'd gladly risk life and limb to succeed?

Sean made a series of turns, and then he sailed off a vertical drop. She held her breath until he landed safely.

"Why the cameras?"

He tipped his wine glass to his mouth and she watched the sexy way his throat muscles worked down a swallow. "Ski documentary." He jerked his chin at the TV. "Here's the good part."

Sean flew down the face, his aggressive turns and speed increasing along with her heart rate. Faster. Snow parted like waves beneath his skis. Faster. His poles barely skimmed the powder. Faster.

Suddenly, he hit a patch of wind-scoured crust and his ski railed out. His body slammed into the mountain face. His skis exploded off his feet, and he tumbled down the slope in a sickening blur of flopping limbs.

She heard a gasp, and when Sean's hand squeezed her arm, she realized the sound had come from her. "It's okay. I was fine. I chose a bad line and paid for it with a few bruises and sprains. And a nasty friction burn on my arm." He twitched a shoulder in a nonchalant shrug. "It happens."

"You could have been killed!"

"Nah, it was nothing. I've had worse." He clicked off the video and switched the TV station to a pop music channel.

"Great. You've had worse, and I'm still trying to catch my breath and I wasn't even there." She shook her head at the insanity. "Do you still do crazy stuff like that?"

He waggled his eyebrows and flashed her a demented grin. "Every chance I get."

Despite the fact that Sean was clearly a loon, his intense

dedication drew her. "Does *anything* scare you?"

"Oh, yeah." He took a drink of wine. "Clowns."

She blinked. "Come again?"

"Clowns," he repeated, shifting so he faced her on the couch. "And corn fields. Corn fields are creepy. I could never live in Nebraska."

"You aren't afraid to leap to your death from a helicopter, but clowns and corn fields scare you?"

"Oh, damn, can you imagine clowns *in* a cornfield?" He shuddered.

She couldn't control the giggle that bubbled up in her throat. "You're weird."

"So I'm brain damaged *and* weird?"

There was laughter in his voice and affection in his eyes as he spoke. He was such a catch, and she began to wonder why she was fighting the attraction. She'd never enjoyed any man's company as much, had never allowed herself to truly relax and laugh. She'd always been on her guard, just waiting for the guy to realize that beneath her diets and workouts she was a whale, and dump her. With Sean, she didn't feel the need to be on her guard...probably because she didn't plan to give him the chance to hurt her.

"You are most definitely both."

On the television, a music video ended, and the familiar voice of the VJ caught her attention. She turned to see George Walker, a video jockey who had taken the music video scene by storm after a short but vibrant stint in radio.

"GeeWiz," she murmured.

"Is the correct response golly gee?"

Excited, she propped her forearms on her knees and leaned toward the TV. "That's GeeWiz. We were friends in college." She slapped her forehead. "I can't believe I didn't think of him sooner."

"Should I be thinking of him as my competition?" he asked in a teasing voice that, to her surprise, sounded a little jealous.

Laughing, she shook her head. "We were just good friends. He dated cheerleaders and sorority flakes." But though he hadn't been interested in Robyn sexually, they'd been close, and he'd always been there for her, ever ready to hunt down and pummel anyone who hurt her.

"You thinking about him for your auction?"

"He'd draw a record crowd."

He gestured to the phone on the table behind the couch. "You can call him now, if you want."

"I've got his number at the hotel. I'll call him when I get back."

"Then let's eat." Sean stood and offered a hand. "Want to join me in the kitchen? Dinner should be ready."

Filled with a renewed sense of hope because she knew George wouldn't let her down, she went with Sean to the kitchen, where he took two round loaves of bread out of the oven. The smell was heavenly...and familiar. As he cut the tops off and scooped out the steaming, tender bread inside, she smiled.

"That's my favorite bread in the world."

"Rosemary cheddar loaves? They make great bowls for the stew. I cheat though. I buy them."

She'd probably made them. "At Hausfreunde. That's what you were going to buy when I saw you there today."

"You caught me." He placed the bread bowls on plates. "I love that place. Their chocolate strudels are the best. The owner always throws in an extra." He gave her a wink. "Probably my wit and charm."

"Could be. My mom has always been a sucker for guys like you."

"Seriously? Your mom owns the bakery?"

"Yep."

"That explains the flour on your face." He cocked his head and studied her for a moment. "Yeah, I see it now. You have the same eyes, same color hair." He winked again. "Your mom's hot."

She socked him in the shoulder. "You're twisted."

"And weird and brain damaged. Want to add anything else to the list?"

"Sexy," she blurted. Horrified, she slapped her hand over her mouth. Had she really said that? Yes, if the sly grin on his face was any clue. No more wine for Robyn.

"There's an adjective I'll take."

He ladled thick, chunky stew into the bowls he'd created and then set the plates on the butcher-block table near the kitchen window. He placed their wine glasses next to the bowls and held out a chair for her. She sat, and he did the same.

"Dig in." He shot her a hungry look that had nothing to do with food. "And save room for dessert."

Chapter Six

Sean watched Robyn eat, surprised and gratified that she wasn't dainty about it. No requests for a salad with low-cal dressing, no complaints that the stew was fattening or that the bread was loaded with carbs. She dug in, making sexy little moans of pleasure.

Now to get her to make sexy little moans of pleasure by other means.

"Do you like chocolate?"

She swallowed a bite of stew. "Are you kidding? Eating good chocolate is practically a religious experience."

"Excellent." He pushed to his feet. "Because I bought a chocolate mint torte at your mom's bakery."

"Oh, you are wicked."

He walked around behind her and leaned over, brushing away her hair from the nape of her neck. "You have no idea," he murmured against the soft, fragrant skin there.

She took a sharp intake of breath. "I think I'm beginning to get one."

A suggestive reply sat on his tongue, but he didn't want to push too hard. Yet. Instead, he started a pot of coffee and placed slices of the rich torte onto two plates. When he set one in front of her, she slid what was left of her stew aside and picked up a fork. For a moment she stared at the dessert, fork hovering above, and then an impish smile turned up one corner of her mouth. Instead of cutting a bite, she slowly, almost lovingly, drew the tip of her finger through the icing.

He got the impression that she didn't often allow herself luxuries like rich desserts. That what he was witnessing was almost a secret ritual, and he watched, feeling like a voyeur but unable to look away, as she dabbed the icing onto her tongue, closing her eyes with a moan that made his mouth go dry.

"Mmm. Tastes like childhood."

A sip of wine moistened his throat so he could speak. "Your parents have always had the bakery?"

She opened her eyes, lit from within by happy memories. "For as long as I can remember. Dad backpacked through Germany during a summer break from law school, and he met my mom at her mother's café. They married, had me and my brothers, moved here, and Mom started up the bakery." She finally cut into the cake and took a bite. "You said you had sisters. Younger? Older?"

"Younger. Shelley and Miranda. Twin terrors who thought it was funny to listen in on my phone conversations and spray my clothes with girly perfume. I used to beg my parents to give them up for adoption."

Robyn put down her fork and braced her forearms on the table. "You don't fool me, Mr. Trenton. You adore them."

He laughed. He did adore them. They were in med school right now, studying to be doctors. Both claimed he inspired their career choice, what with the amount of time they spent nursing him after bad spills on the slopes.

"I suppose they're okay. For sisters."

She gave him a teasing, light swat on the shoulder before picking up her fork again. "They are more than okay. I'll bet you were the big, protective brother all their boyfriends hated."

"Sometimes, I guess." He shrugged. "I wasn't around all that much. They're five years younger, and I was always gone for ski training and competitions."

"What about when there was no snow? What did you do in the summers?"

"I cross-trained in other sports. Kept fit with soccer, cycling, tennis."

"Did you ever have a chance to just have fun?"

There had been plenty of time for partying and women once he moved away from home, but while he'd been under his parents' roof, his life had been dedicated to skiing. "Let's just say that fun was in short supply at times. My dad made sure every spare minute was spent practicing or eating the right foods or thinking winning thoughts."

"Sounds like your parents were pretty supportive. What do they do for a living?"

"My mom is a fourth grade teacher, and my dad coaches college football."

"I'll bet they're proud of you."

He gave a noncommittal nod. His doting mom would be proud of his ability to tie his own shoes. His dad, however, seemed to think he was a failure. No gold, no glory. And worse, no longer perfect, fatally flawed.

Sean had spent years trying to win his father's approval, and during the gold medal years, they'd grown closer. Now his dad could barely look at him.

Though his old man's approval wasn't a priority in his life anymore, he still couldn't help but think that maybe, just maybe, the sports-announcing position would chase the dull haze of disappointment from his father's eyes.

Snowbound

"Coffee's ready," he announced, more to dodge further personal questions than for any other reason. "Want some?"

"Please."

Sean fetched two cups of coffee and returned to the table, where Robyn had propped an elbow and rested her chin in the palm of her hand.

"Thank you for dinner. And for breakfast this morning. And for the short interlude at the bakery. And for saving me yesterday in the bar." She gave a deep, dramatic sigh. "For someone I didn't want to get to know, I've spent a lot of time with you."

"I hope that's not a bad thing."

"It is when I should be hunting for an auction emcee and a job."

The tinge of sadness in her voice pricked his heart. "Is it that hard to find a job in radio?"

"Not usually. The job turnover rate is high. But I've burned some bridges, and I think my ex-boss may have blackballed me."

His stomach tightened like he'd been punched. "Why?"

She hesitated, cut a bite of torte and took her time chewing it. "We used to date back when he was nothing more than a night DJ at the radio station where I worked. Then his dad died, leaving him a lot of shares in the company that owns the station. Damon used his newfound influence to take the most coveted radio spot and to land a regular segment on a Chicago morning show. The size of his ego quadrupled, and we broke up."

He read between the lines there. Damon's newfound fame had opened the door for a lot of hot women, and he'd dumped Robyn to let them in. What an idiot. "So what happened to your job?"

"We worked well together despite the breakup until recently, when he needed a no-strings date for media functions. I did it because he promised to emcee the reunion charity auction, but at the last minute he backed out. When I discovered he lied about the reason for canceling, I lost my temper and quit my job."

"And he retaliated by blackballing you." That son of a bitch. Sean should have trusted his instincts when he'd first met the man.

"I think so. I've been calling all my contacts, and they say there are no jobs open. Not even entry-level positions. And I'm willing to take anything at this point."

The conversation with Damon in which he'd asked Sean to keep Robyn busy in return for giving her a job flashed in his head, and though guilt tore through him at the thought that he was conspiring with the enemy, at least he had an opportunity to make sure Robyn found work.

She covered his hand with her dainty one, and warmth washed over him. "Anyway, I'm sorry I'm such a downer. It's dumb and not your problem."

He shook his head. "It's not dumb, and I want it to be my problem. Can I fix your problem with another slice of torte?"

She laughed, and all traces of sadness dissipated. "Only if you want me groaning and writhing on the floor."

Oh, he wanted her to writhe, and on the floor was fine, as long as she was beneath him. But he wanted her moaning, not groaning.

She studied him over the rim of her coffee cup as she took a sip. "So," she said, putting down the cup, "why did you become an EMT? Was it a childhood dream or something?"

He toyed with her fingers and shook his head. "My childhood dream was to win gold in the Olympics. When those days ended, I couldn't stand the thought of leaving skiing for good, so I became a patroller, and crazily enough, I got a kick out of the medical side of it, so I became an EMT." He brought her hand to his mouth, where he kissed the pulse point in her wrist. "It also gives me something to do in the summer or I'd go stir crazy."

"So I'm guessing money isn't an issue." He liked that she sounded slightly breathless when she spoke.

"Not so much."

Not at all. He had enough saved up from public appearances, product endorsements and TV gigs that he didn't have to work another day in his life. Patrolling and emergency medicine had never been about the money, but about keeping himself busy so he didn't think about all he'd lost.

And the sports announcer job was about regaining a portion of what he'd lost. And speaking of taking back what he'd lost...

"C'mon," he said, standing. "I rented a couple of movies. Do you like James Bond?"

"Doesn't everyone?"

Damn, this woman could grow on him. He took her hand and led her to the living room, but before they made it to the couch, she stopped and gave him an apologetic look. "Where did you say the bathroom was?"

"Upstairs and to the left."

"Thanks." She disappeared up the stairs, her fine backside swinging provocatively.

He popped a movie into the DVD player and added a couple of logs to the fire in the wood stove. He didn't have a plan of attack, but he did know he wanted to win Robyn over, make her forget about his very public past. Strangely enough, this was no longer about getting laid just to push past his insecurities.

Well, it *was* about that, but it was also about just being with her. He actually *liked* her. That she wanted to talk about anything but the one subject women always wanted to discuss—his skiing success—was strangely refreshing. As was the fact that he'd been forced to pursue her, something he'd never really done. The chase had been fun, a burning challenge he welcomed because he hadn't been challenged by anything in a long, long time, and suddenly now there was life at the end of the tunnel.

He dimmed the lights and looked up as Robyn started down the stairs.

As always, the sight of her took away his breath and left him feeling like he needed a hit of oxygen from his medic kit. This time, though, he had a hard time catching it again. Her legs, encased in dark denim, seemed to go on forever, from her stockinged feet all the way up to her generous hips. Her fuzzy blue sweater hid her waist, which he knew to be perfectly made for his hands. His gaze traveled up, lingered on her full breasts he was sure would be just as suited for his touch.

And her neck...long, delicate, with a pulse beneath the creamy skin that picked up in tempo as he stared. She halted on the bottom step, putting her at eye level with him and just a foot away. The air moving between those twelve inches sizzled.

"You started the movie," she said in a husky voice that settled low and deep in his belly.

"Can't get much by you."

She swallowed and licked her lips, and damn if he didn't get hard right then and there. "Sean Connery. He's my favorite."

"Mine too."

Her green eyes darkened. "He's so sexy."

Tension coiled inside him, and he took a step closer so they were almost touching. "Not my type."

She nodded, and her gaze dropped to his mouth. "His lips...tempting."

She didn't know what tempting was. Tempting was a beautiful woman standing a mere inch away, her sweet fragrance tickling his nostrils. Tempting was the way her breasts rose and fell with her rapidly increasing breaths.

He was tired of being tempted. He wanted to take. He framed her face in his hands and stroked his thumb over the silky skin of her cheeks. A low moan sounded deep in Robyn's chest and she closed her eyes, for once not protesting his touch. He leaned in until he could feel her breath, warm and damp, on his skin, could almost taste the building storm of anticipation that roiled between them.

Unable to wait any longer, he pressed his lips to hers, which parted for him and ensured that any control he had left sped away like skis after a bad fall.

The taste of her, mint and chocolate and sin, nearly brought him to his knees. Cupping the back of her head with one hand, he pulled her closer to feel the soft curves of her body against his chest, his stomach, his groin.

Her soft, questing hands slipped beneath his sweatshirt and spread wide on his back, caressing and kneading, and then dropping to his buttocks. She squeezed so that her short, strong nails dug into his ass cheeks, wringing a ragged groan from him.

Her tongue curved against his, sucking lightly and thrusting deep, matching his passion stroke for stroke. Desperate to stoke that passion even higher, hotter, he ran a hand down her side and then back up until his thumb met the underside of her breast. He smoothed his fingers along the line of her bra, and when he gently squeezed her breast, she gasped.

The sound pulsed through him with a buzz he'd like to blame on the wine, but he knew better. Robyn was more potent than any alcohol, more addictive, for sure.

His palm drifted down her trim waist, along her softly rounded hip to her thigh, which he then lifted to his waist. He brought her other leg up as well, so that her long limbs were wrapped around his torso, her arms around his neck. Now to get her into this same position while being horizontal...

Sean took a step back, intent upon settling on the couch. His calf struck something soft—something that meowed indignantly, and he suddenly had to catch his balance. He barely avoided stepping on Norbert as he stumbled to the wall next to the stairs. Holding Robyn with one arm, he extended the other to keep her back from slamming against the wall.

"Sorry," he muttered, wincing. *Smooth, Trenton. Real smooth.* James Bond he was not.

Robyn tightened her legs around his waist and kissed a path from his mouth to his ear, where she teased the lobe with a gentle suck. "Just keep kissing me. Please."

As if she'd needed to beg. Sandwiching her between his body and the wall, he took her mouth with renewed enthusiasm as her fingers stabbed through his hair and her tongue met his with eager velvet strokes.

His erection nudged the junction between her legs, and she whimpered, ground against it, searing him from the inside out. Her heat cradled his cock and his brain fogged, and all he could do was ride the motion with her until they were both panting and he'd forgotten why sex had ever become an issue for him.

"Sean...mmm, yes, keep doing that—" She broke off to kiss him deeply, fiercely.

Crushing her more firmly against the wall, he freed his hands to support her weight around his waist, though he probably didn't need to. She glommed onto him with strong, tightly clenched thighs, her movements as frenzied as his own.

His skin tightened and burned beneath her fingers until the soft cotton of his clothing felt like torture. He tore off his sweatshirt and her sweater, frantic to feel hot flesh on hot flesh. When he looked down at her, at how her pale skin contrasted with the black satin bra, his heart thundered in his chest as though trying to get closer to hers. He wasn't sure he could get close enough.

She arched in invitation, and with one deft flick of his fingers, the front clasp of the bra clicked open, allowing him full access to her lightly freckled, full breasts.

His breath caught when he looked into her face and saw her eyes, slumberous and smoldering, watching him. "Touch me, Sean."

"Yes." His voice sounded coarse and foreign, reminding him how long it had been since he'd been with a woman.

Greedy hope surged through his veins, urging him on. He dipped his head, brought his mouth down on her swollen lips.

Her skin scorched his palm as he cupped a breast and skimmed his thumb over a pebbled nipple. A low moan deep in her chest told him what he'd just done to her, and the increased rhythmic speed of the thrust of her hips told him how excited she was. He knew the feeling, because he himself was at the very brink.

God, this was real. He was really going to do it. He was going to lick every inch of her body and then bury himself in her slick, hot heat.

He kept kissing her, this exquisite, sexy woman who pushed all his buttons, who smelled of vanilla and berries and her own special scent that drove him mad. He wanted to drive her mad too, wanted to see her come apart in his arms.

Dropping his hands, he lifted her buttocks, tilting her more fully against his cock as he thrust between her legs in slow, easy motions. Sweat beaded on his forehead and his thighs quivered. He'd have to stop this or lose it, but it felt so good, so natural to be here with her like this.

"There," she moaned against his lips. "Oh, God, there."

She threw her head back against the wall and shuddered, cried out his name as she came. Nothing had ever sounded so wonderful, looked so beautiful as Robyn Montgomery in her release, and he wanted to make it happen again and again.

Her eyes fluttered open and he met her gaze, seeing a haze of passion that took his breath away. "Take me upstairs," she whispered.

Her legs slid down his until she was on her feet, swaying slightly. She shrugged out of the bra that had been hanging off her shoulders and closed the narrow gap between them. It was erotic as hell, the way she stood there, naked from the waist up, and it only became more so when she trailed her hands down his heaving, damp chest, over his stomach, and to the waistband of his jeans. She pressed a pattern of kisses along his throat and down his shoulder as she worked the button and unzipped his fly.

The first stirrings of panic wrapped around him as she reached into his boxers and took his cock in her palm. *It's okay, it's okay*, he told himself over and over, but still, he grabbed her wrist as if to stop her mind-blowing caress. Undeterred, she kept working him, her warm hand squeezing and moving in precise, firm strokes, holding him captive. He couldn't move a muscle, and wasn't sure if he wanted to.

Even his throat muscles had frozen, because when he tried

to speak, it came out as more of a raspy croak. "Robyn, stop, or we won't make it upstairs."

A wicked smile curved her lips, and she didn't stop. "I don't need a bed." Her other hand joined the first, one rubbing, stroking until he thought he'd die.

Pleasure pulsed upward under her skilled fingers, and he looked down to see a bead of precome form at the tip of his penis. He was close, so close his legs had become rubbery and he had to grasp her shoulders for balance. Still smiling, she drew her thumb over the drop of moisture and used the pad of one finger to spread it around the glans.

The slippery friction was magic, beyond anything he could have hoped for tonight. His fingers dug into Robyn's shoulders as one of her hands pumped him to the very edge, and the other eased lower, lower, down to—

"No," he said gruffly. "Stop." He jerked her hand away from him and stepped back, panting, his hands shaking. He suddenly felt like the crazy person she'd already accused him of being.

She blinked, her eyes unfocused and confused. "I'm sorry. I, um...Sean, what's wrong?"

Oh, hell. What's wrong? He'd just blown his shot at getting laid tonight, that's what. Even worse, he'd probably screwed up his chances of building some kind of relationship with Robyn.

His heart seized. When, exactly, had a relationship become a goal? Damn, but he was an idiot. This was about sex. It was about getting off. End of story.

And he still managed to mess it up. The one thing besides skiing and emergency medicine he'd ever been good at.

"I'm sorry." He zipped up, but he couldn't look her in the eye. He could barely look in her direction. "I'm, uh, shy."

"You honestly expect me to believe that?"

"It would be helpful."

He glanced over at her, and instantly wished he hadn't. She gave him a hard stare that told him she wasn't going to fall for any lines or be distracted by humor. He blew out a breath. "Look, it's my fault. It's me, not you."

She wrapped her arms around herself as if she were cold, but he suspected she was covering her breasts, feeling exposed and embarrassed. "It isn't me," she murmured. "Guys always say that when they dump you. 'It's not you, it's me.' What does that mean?"

Guilt plowed over Sean like a runaway snow groomer. He knew exactly what she was talking about. He'd used that line on women in the past. What did it mean? *Thanks for the good time, babe, but I've gotten my fill of you, and I'm moving on to untracked snow.*

But that wasn't the case in this situation, and somehow he had to convince her.

"Robyn, I'm not trying to ditch you." He took her hand, started to lead her to the couch, but she dug in her heels and shook her head.

"Take me home." She snatched her hand from his to gather her bra and sweater. "To the lodge."

"Not until we talk about this. I need to explain." Not that he knew what to say. He only knew the truth wasn't an option.

She turned away from him and pulled her sweater over her head. "I don't want to hear it." The silence grew thick while she smoothed her sweater several times before turning back to him and shoving the bra into her jeans' pocket. "Just drive me back."

"Robyn—"

"Now."

She stalked to her boots and jammed her feet into them without giving him another look. He just stared as she shrugged into her coat and waited, tapping one booted foot and gazing at the ceiling.

Finally, with a sigh, he put on his boots and coat and grabbed his keys.

And he'd thought the date so many months ago with Jenny had ended badly.

Chapter Seven

"Men suck."

Karen put down her peppermint-schnapps-spiked hot cocoa and cocked a blonde eyebrow at Robyn's profound observation. "You could make a killing if you put that on a bumper sticker." A candy cane stir stick hung on the inside edge of her cup, and she absently swirled it through the drink, her expression growing serious. "So you guys didn't say a word on the drive back to the lodge? Nothing?"

"Nada."

As they'd driven along dark mountain roads, she'd thought Sean was going to speak once when he took a deep breath and his hands tightened on the steering wheel. But eventually he relaxed and pressed his lips together, letting the silence grow even louder with the echoes of what he didn't say.

Not even music had played on his state-of-the-art stereo system that seemed so out of place in the ancient SUV.

She blew steam off the surface of her coffee and cast a glance out of BrewSki restaurant's large front window overlooking the mountain's western face. The runs were crowded, too crowded for her taste. The ski competition had the resort hopping, which had been more than enough of an excuse to take a lunch break from skiing. Well, it was a break for Karen, but Robyn had to head out soon. Her mother wanted her help at the bakery.

"Why didn't you let him explain?"

Robyn set down her mug, wrapping her fingers around it for warmth. "Explain what? That I don't turn him on? That I don't fawn all over his Olympic medal enough?"

"From what you've said, I doubt any of those things are an issue." Karen hid a smile in her cup. "Especially the turning-on part."

Robyn knew that, knew she wasn't being fair. There was no doubt in her mind that he'd been as turned on as she'd been. She'd felt the evidence in her hand and between her legs. And the Olympic medal thing definitely wasn't a concern. He hadn't brought up his sports career and fame once.

Then again, maybe he expected her to talk about it, and when she didn't...

"Speak of the devil?"

Robyn's head whipped around, and she searched the crowded pub for a tall hunk in a red jacket. "Where?"

"Outside."

She turned to the window and saw him. There, standing by the quad lift in his ski patrol gear, ruffling the hair of a small red-headed boy. Sean's sunglasses hid his eyes, but even from this distance, the dazzling smile on his face mesmerized her and made feathery wings flit around inside her belly. She couldn't decide if she should be happy to see him smiling or upset that he wasn't as miserable as she was.

Then the boy skied away, and Sean's smile faded. He speared his hand through his streaky brown and blond hair and threw his head back to the sunny sky. So maybe he *was* as miserable as she had been since she'd stepped out of his truck and slammed the door. Somehow the knowledge didn't make her feel any better.

Last night had been so perfect at first, the environment relaxed, the conversation never awkward. And when he'd kissed her on the stairs, she'd allowed all her personal insecurities and fears about his past and future to disappear so she could enjoy the moment. She hadn't intended for things to go as far as they had—or would have. But once his hands were on her, she'd given in to the attraction she'd felt since she'd first seen him sitting on the bar stool in the Moosehead, looking like her high school fantasy come alive.

What a colossal mistake.

Outside, Sean tugged on his glove and headed toward another patroller who beckoned him from near a lift where a crowd had gathered around several camera crews. The resort had always been a popular hangout for the paparazzi and television reporters, but since she'd arrived it seemed she couldn't turn around without running into some form of media. Fortunately, she'd been spared another run-in with Damon and his station team.

Sean seemed to take the photographers in stride, flashing them smiles and waves as he skied past. With a sigh she wasn't sure signaled weariness or desire, she turned back to Karen, who eyed her with concern.

"You fell for him, didn't you?"

"Of course not," Robyn scoffed, reaching for a stuffed potato skin a server had delivered while she'd been pining for Sean. She was going to have to live on celery and carrot sticks for a month after this vacation. "I've known him, what? Two days?"

"Time isn't an issue when it comes to love."

Robyn snorted. Her friend was such a romantic. "Lust, not love. I'll admit there's a fair amount of the former involved, but the latter? Get real. I'm not making that mistake again."

"What mistake? You were never in love with Damon." Karen froze as she lifted her mug to her mouth. "Were you?"

Still holding the uneaten potato skin, Robyn flopped back in her seat. She thought she'd loved Damon at one time, but now she realized she'd been in love with the idea of love. But even though she hadn't loved him, not really, he'd still hurt her. Over and over...and she'd let him, which made the pain even worse. The self-inflicted kind always hurt the most.

"I wasn't in love with him. But I did care for him. So seeing him all over the place, on TV and on billboards...it just rubs salt in the wound. Can you imagine how magnified that pain would be if I fell for Sean and he ended up famous again?"

"But you said he'd given up on that."

Robyn's gaze drifted to the far wall, where a glossy poster of a much younger Sean standing on a medalist podium hung in a position of prominence. His expression, self-assured and ecstatic, made her gut do a slow, pleasant roll even now.

Lord, she had it bad.

She scooped a dab of sour cream off her potato skin and sucked it off her finger. "He has."

"Then you're seeing trouble where there is none."

"You don't think him breaking things off in the middle of some pretty serious action isn't trouble?"

"You didn't give him a chance to explain."

Robyn glared at her friend. "Whose side are you on?"

As irritated as Robyn was, she couldn't come close to matching the look Karen seared her with. "Yours. But come on. I know you. You get freaked out and start inventing worst-case scenarios before you get all the facts."

"So what do you think his excuse is?"

Shrugging, Karen took a sip of cocoa. "I dunno. Maybe he's impotent."

Robyn thought about how hard he'd been when she wrapped her hand around him. "No, definitely not impotent."

"Do you think he's got some sort of premature ejaculation thing going on?"

She eyed Karen skeptically. *"Premature ejaculation?"*

Strangled coughs exploded around her, and she cast a sheepish glance at the four guys at the next table. She turned back and lowered her voice. "No way."

Absolutely not. She recalled how he'd held onto his control while she lost hers, and she had to force herself to ignore the dull ache of desire the memory sparked. But then, right afterward, she'd barely touched him and he jerked away...

She pursed her lips and slid Karen a hesitant glance. "Really? You think?"

"I have no idea," Karen said, finally reaching for a potato skin. "Why don't you just ask?"

"Oh. Sure. Guys love it when you come right out and ask if they sell the wine before its time."

"Stop being difficult. I'm sure he has a logical excuse." She jerked her thumb at the four guys from earlier, who were ogling a group of women who'd just walked through the door. "I mean, what guy would turn down a chance to have sex without a really good reason? Give the man a chance to explain."

Robyn considered her friend's words. She had, after all, cut him off when he tried to do just that. It was habit. Guys had shot her down years ago because of her weight, so she'd become accustomed to closing up before they could give her the "it's not you, it's me" pity speech. She'd responded out of instinct last night. Instinct and hurt and humiliation. Her face still burned when she thought about how easily her body had succumbed to a little pelvic grinding.

Still, something told her Sean hadn't deserved what she'd done, that he was different from other guys despite the fact that he could have any woman he wanted and probably *had* had every woman he wanted. Yet this man who jumped out of helicopters into mountainside deathtraps had chosen to pursue her even though her idea of taking risks was to ski and chew gum at the same time.

So had that been the reason he'd broken things off so suddenly? She hadn't proved exciting enough? Damon had said something similar once, that she was too "reserved".

Well, no more. For once, she needed to let go. Throw caution to the wind. Sean had said he was finished with competitive skiing and groupies and with being in the spotlight. He said he wanted her. So for once in her life, she was going to trust that and take a risk. She was going to take care of her reunion and job troubles and have her fling.

For the first time ever, the view from the summit, the sight of the sun glistening off of hoar-frosted fir that rose out of unspoiled snow, failed to move Sean. And for the first time, as he made his way down the slope, he failed to get in touch with the Zen of carving.

He'd screwed up badly last night and embarrassment stung him with the ferocity of an icy wind. Robyn probably thought he was either an idiot or that he wasn't attracted to her, and while the jury was still out on the former, the latter couldn't be

115

further from the truth.

He was more attracted to her than he'd ever been to anyone, and it went beyond the surface, beyond beauty and physique. Something more, something deep inside her had taken hold of him, had touched him somewhere deep inside himself. Conflicting emotions and thoughts swirled through him, tugging at above-the-belt organs that weren't accustomed to dealing with women. What the hell was happening to him?

Cursing, he straightened his skis and crouched, increasing his speed in a bid to outrun his confusion and irritation, and left Todd, to whom he'd barely spoken today, well behind. He skidded to a stop midway down the run to dress down two teenaged boys who were skiing recklessly, endangering more well-behaved guests. The mountain cop routine worked out a little of the tension that had him wound up tighter than his boot bindings, and by the time he hit the bottom of the run, he felt marginally better.

Better, that was, until Todd caught up with him.

"You out of your funk yet?"

"I'm not in a funk."

"You're so deep in funk you reek." Todd looked out at the ocean of skiers milling about and waved at someone he knew. "Your little radio honey didn't give it up last night, did she?"

Sean squinted in the bright sunlight at his partner. "Do you ever think of anything else?"

"When did you *stop* thinking of anything else?"

Good question. And one to which Sean had no answer. Well, not entirely true. Drinking and partying and one-night stands had taken a backseat to surgery and physical rehabilitation and healing two years ago, and he'd never really brought the elements he'd considered so important to the front seat again.

Reintroducing those elements into his life once more was what he'd hoped to accomplish with the commentator job and getting laid.

Funny, but getting laid didn't seem so important now. Oh, he wanted to spend a couple of hot, sweaty hours in bed with a woman, but he wanted that woman to be Robyn. Only Robyn. And he wanted more than a meaningless fuck.

Maybe that was the problem. His goal had been simply to get her into bed, just as it had been with Jenny. But Jenny had been a port in a storm who wanted nothing more than a mutually satisfying good time, and when he'd freaked out at the last minute, she'd reacted...badly.

Robyn was more than that, definitely not the fling type, and yet he'd been treating her like one. No, not exactly. Sure, everything he'd said and done had been carefully designed to get her into bed, but he'd also taken her home instead of to a hotel. He'd cooked dinner instead of taking her out to a fancy restaurant. He'd rented movies instead of going to one.

So obviously Robyn was more to him than a fling, but he'd failed to see that. Maybe he needed to develop a real relationship with her. Maybe he needed to ease into a place where he felt comfortable making love to her instead of merely screwing.

Maybe he was turning into a big fucking sap.

"Earth to Sean."

Sean blinked at the gloved hand waving in front of his eyes. "What?"

"Let's grab a cup of coffee and work out a new plan."

Sean jammed his poles into the snow to push off. "Coffee, yes. Plan, no. I've already got one."

He was going to do things differently for once. A unique

plan for a unique woman and a unique situation. He was going to go slow. And he'd start by telling her the truth about the sports announcer job. For once in his life, he was going to have a relationship. Not a fling.

✳ ✳ ✳

Robyn had barely finished squeezing the filling into a strawberry tartlet when her cell phone's muffled ring made her stomach lurch with a combination of anticipation and dread. She'd gotten a job lead after lunch, she'd made a follow-up call to another potential employer and she'd left a message on Sean's home answering machine. *Oh, please, please, let it be good news.*

Quickly, she grabbed a towel and wiped her hands as she ran to the bakery's tiny office to dig through her purse. She snagged the cell phone on the fourth ring and her heart pounded crazily when she looked at the name flashing on the phone's screen.

George Walker, alias GeeWiz, returning the desperate call she'd made to him last night in the hotel room after leaving Sean. At the time, he'd had no job leads for her, but he'd promised to do his best to help her out with the auction, and hopefully his help involved him flying to Colorado to emcee.

Hand shaking, she put the phone to her ear.

"Hey, babe," George purred in the deep voice that had propelled him to fame.

"George. *Please* tell me you have good news."

A long pause stretched out over the airwaves and her spark of hope fizzled. "Yes and no. I'm sorry, but I can't make it there to emcee. My agent booked me for an awards dinner I can't back out of."

Disappointment sucked the strength from her bones and she sank heavily into the office chair. "That's all right," she managed, even though it wasn't. "It was a long shot."

"Yeah, total bummer. If I'd known sooner...but it isn't all bad." His voice took an upbeat swing. "I got you a bunch of stuff for the auction. Some signed CDs and DVDs by top artists, some prereleases, promotional T-shirts, gift certificates for our online shop and a karaoke machine. I'll have everything overnighted. Does that help?"

Tears of both gratitude and frustration welled in her eyes. George couldn't make it like she'd hoped, but the items he'd procured would help the money-raising effort. "Oh, George, I don't know how to thank you."

"Just be a success, babe. You deserve it. Damon isn't fit to breathe the same air as you, so don't let him get to you."

She thanked George again—as well as she could through the sobs that clogged her throat, and hung up. Now what? George had been her last, best hope.

She slumped forward and banged her head on the desk. How was she going to break the news to the reunion committee? She'd volunteered to organize the auction, and because of her contacts with radio celebs, they'd asked her to arrange an emcee. Of course she'd jumped right up and agreed so she could show off her success and finally impress the people who had made her teenage years absolute hell.

Now she was going to hand them the hammer to pound in the last nail in her coffin. To save the auction, she might be forced to do what she'd said so casually to Damon—emcee herself. The thought made her want to curl into a quivering ball on the floor. Not only was she near-phobic about crowds and being in front of them, but she wouldn't draw the number of people they'd need to bring in a lot of money. The auction was going to go down on her high school's list of most gargantuan failures.

Because of her.

"Robyn?"

She lifted her head and looked at her mom through blurry eyes. "Yes?"

Her mother bustled into the office. "Honey, what's wrong?"

Sitting up, Robyn grabbed a tissue from the box on the desk. "Nothing. I've just got some job issues."

She felt bad about lying—well, she *did* have job issues, but they weren't her major concern at the moment. Her mom simply would not understand the reunion thing. Because Robyn's academic record had been flawless in high school, her mother had not been sympathetic to her social troubles. She figured that since Robyn got good grades, nothing else should bother her.

"What kind of job issues?"

Robyn hesitated. Her family would be so disappointed if they knew the truth. She'd bragged about her success, about how happy she was as a big city girl and with the money she made. And now she was paying for her boastful ways.

"Piles and piles of work."

"Then this vacation must be good for you."

Yeah, right. Robyn smiled and hoped she didn't look sick.

"Sweetie," her mom began, pulling up a seat, "we need to talk."

By "talk", her mother meant "the end of the world is at hand". She braced herself for whatever bomb her mom was about to drop.

"I've told you your father hasn't been helping much with

the bakery anymore, yes?"

Robyn nodded.

"He bought a hunting cabin. You remember Mr. Delaney's place?"

How could she forget the cozy four-room cabin near the lodge where her family used to ride in on horseback and stay for hunting and fishing weekends? Mr. Delaney had been a family friend until he died last year, and he'd allowed the Montgomerys use the cabin anytime they wished. The memories of time spent at the cabin were as precious to her as those she had of helping her parents at the bakery.

"Why would he buy a cabin?" An acid glob sank to the pit of her belly, and she grasped the edge of the desk as though she might fall over. "You aren't...you wouldn't get a divorce?"

Her mom laughed and laid a hand on her knee. "Oh, heavens no. Your dad bought it so he can start a business as a hunting guide."

Relief flooded her, but she remained tense. "Why?"

"We're ready to retire. The hunting guide thing is a little something to keep your father busy. You know how he is." Her mother's German accent thickened—a telltale sign of stress. "So we're selling Hausfreunde."

"What? No!" She shook her head. She couldn't have heard that right. But one look at her mother's dour expression said otherwise. "No. You can't do that!"

"It's time. We don't want to be making *lebküchen* in our wheelchairs."

"You aren't that old," Robyn protested.

"No, but we want to enjoy ourselves before we *are* that old."

"Couldn't Joe or Greg—"

Her mother clucked her tongue and sighed. "Greg is too

busy with the airline to care about the bakery. And Joe...well, he's Joe."

Robyn nodded in understanding. Neither brother had a clean track record when it came to reliability, but at least Greg was making a good life as a pilot for a private charter company. Joe had no idea what he wanted out of life except to have a good time, and being saddled with a responsibility like Hausfreunde was more horse than he could handle.

"Your father and I were hoping you'd want to take over."

Robyn's first impulse was to hug her mother for knowing how much the bakery meant to her. Her second impulse was to scream at her for not realizing how cruel the offer was. Hausfreunde had always been a source of comfort, but it had also been a source of food she couldn't resist. How could she possibly spend all her time here without eating everything she could get her hands on? No way. She'd worked too hard to lose weight and get healthy, and she couldn't risk succumbing to the temptation of comfort food again.

Sure, she'd been able to resist so far, but visiting and helping was one thing. Working at the bakery on a daily basis was another. Especially in a city filled with beautiful people. Often famous people. A city where her peers had been vicious. And where she'd probably run into Sean regularly. What if that impulse to binge became a demon she couldn't control? She'd blow up like a hot air balloon.

"I can't do it, Mom."

"But—"

"No."

The warm scent of baking bread wafted into the office as an employee walked past the open door, and Robyn's stomach soured. Losing the bakery would be like losing a family member.

She felt like a huge piece of her heart had been ripped from her chest. Things around her were spinning out of control and sliding downhill fast. She could use a rescue from a sexy ski patroller right about now. More than ever she wanted to see Sean, to sink into his embrace and feel nothing but *him*.

Hopefully he'd forgive her for her behavior last night, because she desperately needed a distraction, an intense escape that would make her forget everything. And for once, she'd make the first move. She'd call him, ask him to meet her tomorrow. This time, she was going to take some risks, because really, she had nothing left to lose.

Chapter Eight

Sean was nervous. *Nervous.* Before he met Robyn in the bar the other day, he could count on one hand the number of times he'd suffered from a case of nerves unrelated to ski competitions. Now he couldn't get rid of the heart palpitations and churning stomach, which only grew worse as he prepared to meet her in the warming house at the top of Frost Run—the first time he'd be seeing her since the disaster at his house the night before last.

He'd gone to Robyn's room yesterday after he got off work, but she hadn't been there, so he'd sped home, where he'd found two messages on his answering machine. The first, from his agent, Samantha, said how eager she was to see his career take off again, even if it was taking off in a direction none had expected. Though she'd had no specific details, she'd mentioned the possibility of some exciting news soon.

The message sounded promising, exactly what he'd wanted but had been afraid to hope for. Ditto on the second message. That one had been from Robyn. Her sexy, sultry voice still echoed through his head and filled him with a surge of hopeful anticipation.

"Hi, Sean...it's Robyn. Look, um...I'm sorry I was such a jerk the other night. I'd love to talk if you have a minute. Call me?"

He hadn't been able to punch the buttons on his handset fast enough. She'd been in her room, had answered in a strong, professional voice—probably in case the call had been from a potential employer—but her tone had softened when she realized he was on the other end of the line. The conversation had been short, and they'd agreed to meet at the warming house after he got off work.

So here he was, riding the Green Line lift in a light snow. The National Weather Service hadn't predicted it to worsen much with the approaching frontal system, but his old leg injury was aching, and he'd long ago learned to listen. The front was going to bring some hellish weather. He'd seen how conditions on the mountain could deteriorate from mild to severe in a matter of minutes, and the throbbing just below his knee told him it was only a matter of time.

At the landing, he shoved off the chair and skied to the warming house, where he left his skis and poles in the designated area. Warm air blasted his frozen face as he opened the door, and then he saw Robyn seated on a wooden bench near the central fireplace, and the warmth seeped all the way to his bones.

She combed her fingers through cinnamon hair that was slightly mashed from the purple fleece hat on the table. She'd removed her jacket, revealing a red turtleneck that matched her cheeks, still ruddy from the cold.

She didn't see him at first, not until a local skier spotted him and gave a hearty shout. "Trenton! Hey, good to see you!"

It seemed like everyone in the place turned, including Robyn. Sean nodded a greeting to the guy and clomped across the boot-scuffed wooden floor, his stomach flip-flopping like it hadn't since his competition days.

Robyn watched his approach, her expression wary, as

though she was trying as hard to get a read on his mood as he was trying to get one on hers.

"Hi," he said, unsure if he should take a seat.

She smiled. Thank God. He wouldn't have blamed her if she'd thrown her hot drink on him and stormed out.

"Hi, yourself." She glanced at his patrol jacket. "I thought you said you'd meet me when you got off."

He bit his tongue. He could take that sentence to a million places, but now definitely wasn't the time or place.

"I am off work. I just didn't want to take the time to change. I couldn't wait to see you."

"Really?"

"Yeah."

Both her smile and the color in her cheeks deepened, and she gestured to the bench across from her. "Have a seat."

So far, so good. She didn't hate him, at least. "Thanks."

"Can I order something for you? Coffee? Something to eat?"

"I'm fine."

He watched her tease a manicured fingernail around the rim of her mug, and his body clenched at the memory of how those same nails had dug into his skin in the heat of passion.

He waited through one deep, steadying breath before bracing his forearms on the table and leaning forward to say, "Look, I'm sorry about the other night—"

"Don't," she said, reaching to take his hand across the distance that suddenly felt like miles and not inches. He wanted to be sitting *with* her, not across from her. "It's okay."

He looked around the busy establishment and lowered his voice. "It's not okay. I screwed up."

"That's the thing," she began, shaking her head. "You didn't screw up. I did. I've been sending mixed signals, telling you I don't want anything to happen between us, and then jumping all over you."

"Let me assure you that you jumping all over me is *not* a problem."

She laughed, that pure, rich sound he'd become addicted to, that gave him a buzz no alcohol could match. "Good. Because no more mixed signals. I'm tired of playing it safe and trying to protect myself."

Her smile faded. Lips pressed together tightly, she stared him in the eye, her own eyes flashing green sparks in the firelight. "My job forces me to deal with record execs, TV and radio producers, celebrities and high-strung disc jockeys. On a work level, no one intimidates me. I'm good at my job, and I'm aggressive. I take no prisoners."

He cocked his head, suddenly able to see the smart *über*-shark inside the cuddly ski bunny, and a new appreciation for her tumbled over him like an avalanche. Only a few days had passed since they'd met, and already he had discovered complex layers inside her that no woman in his past had possessed.

Or maybe they had, but he'd been too self-absorbed to notice.

"But?"

"Buuuut," she drawled, "I've been a wimp in my personal life. Total spineless jellyfish. Marshmallow."

"Marshmallow?"

She nodded. "And not even the stale, firm kind. The fresh, super-soft kind."

He squeezed her hand. "I'm sure it wasn't that bad."

"Oh, it was that bad. But no more. I've taken a lot of

business risks and not one has backfired." She caught her lip between her teeth again, hard enough that he wanted to soothe it with his tongue. "Well, there is the quitting and blackballing, but that's different. My point is that risks work for me in business, but playing it safe in my personal life has been a colossal failure, so it's time for a change. It's time to jump in with both feet."

A sense of relief washed over him. He, too, was ready to jump in with both feet. There was still that pesky matter of his...disfigurement, but he'd deal with that when the time came.

He felt like he'd just broken a season-long losing streak and now had a shot at gold. Grinning like a fool, he drew her hand to his mouth and kissed her palm. "Sounds like we're on the same page. And there's something I need to talk to you about, so what do you say we start with dinner?"

A dangerous combination of heat and mischief darkened her eyes, and she offered a sly smile. "Too safe. I was thinking we should start with dessert."

"That does sound dangerous," he teased. "Do you think we'll shock the waiter when we order cheesecake before the main course?"

She frowned. "Um, I meant—"

"Robyn!"

They both turned to see Karen thumping toward them, whipping her snow-crusted hat off her head. She stopped at the table and gave Sean a quick, breathless hello before turning to Robyn.

"I've been trying to reach you on your cell, but you haven't answered."

Robyn rolled her eyes. "Stupid thing doesn't work on the mountain. What's up?"

"A guy named Mike Anderson called from Los Angeles about a job at KREX."

"Oh my God! What did he say?"

"That you need to call him tomorrow morning between eight and noon or he's going to give the job to some guy from Sacramento."

Robyn bounced in her seat with excitement. "You're kidding!"

"And that's not all." Karen stretched out a dramatic pause long enough that Sean thought Robyn might explode with anticipation before adding, "He's heard through the grapevine that you need an announcer for your auction, and if you get hold of him in the morning he'll see if he can schedule Donny J. to do it."

For a moment, Robyn looked shell shocked, beautifully shell shocked, and even more so when she let out a whoop so loud everyone in the establishment turned to stare. She didn't care, just grinned like she'd won the lottery.

"Donny J.," she said with a giddiness that suited her, "is L.A.'s most popular morning DJ."

Sean nodded. "I've heard of him." He'd actually been interviewed by the obnoxious DJ, but he didn't feel the need to share that with Robyn.

"I hope everyone here has heard of him, too. He guest spots on some of the music video channels sometimes." She drummed her fingers on the table. "Hmm, this could work out even better than if Damon had done it."

It'd probably irritate the hell out of him to know that Robyn had gotten a job without his help and in spite of his blackballing. Worse, she'd landed an emcee who was a hundred times more famous than Damon.

Pleased with the image that presented and thrilled for Robyn, he smiled. "Congratulations. Wanna celebrate?"

"Dessert?"

"Anything you want."

Robyn leaned across the table, so close their lips nearly touched, and her lids went to half-mast as her gaze burned into his. "Anything?" she purred, in a low, seductive voice that made heat pool in his groin.

He swallowed dryly. "Yep."

"Then I know the perfect thing to get the adrenaline flowing."

✳ ✳ ✳

Sheer, explosive pleasure burst through Robyn as she hurtled down The Dark Side. Snowflakes stung her face, but goggles protected her eyes from the worst of the weather, and her mood shielded her from the rest.

Finally, she'd gotten a break. A job and an auction emcee were within her grasp, and she had a hot night with Sean planned for the evening. A hot night to accompany her new change in attitude. No more safety net. She was taking the plunge, both with Sean and on the slope.

She turned sharply to avoid a hip-high mogul that Sean, slightly ahead of her, had jumped with a casual recklessness that seemed to define the man.

She wasn't going to go *that* crazy in her quest to add some excitement in her life, but she *had* elected to ski a very advanced slope, and with more aggression and confidence than she'd ever dreamed of. She cast a quick glance behind her. Karen, too, had avoided the mogul. Smart girl. Leave the suicide jumps to loonies like Sean.

When she looked forward again, she nearly ran into him. He'd braked to help a wiped-out skier to her feet. Robyn veered away in a spray of snow and shouted on her way past, "Meet you at Après Ski!"

He gave her a thumbs-up, and she barreled down the slope, took a curve so fast she swore her organs switched places. Terror and triumph collided in a bolt of ecstasy that ripped the breath from her lungs. Now she understood some of what Sean experienced when he jumped from helicopters and plunged down steep tracts of boulder-strewn mayhem. The adrenaline rush careened through her bloodstream, propelling her to new heights and unaccustomed levels of invincibility.

Then Karen passed her, and she realized she was still holding back a little, that she hadn't broken through all her barriers.

"Come on!" Karen shouted back, slowing. "Let's beat him to the bottom!"

"You do remember that he used to make a living by beating people to the bottom of mountains, right?"

"We can take a shortcut."

Her friend came to a hard stop near the edge of the slope. Snow swirled around a sign that pointed to a narrower run, one of the resort's Suicide Chutes. The chutes were shortcuts to other runs, mid-mountain warming houses or winter fun centers. They delivered the adventure of the backcountry without the extreme danger. During the summer, they became trails for hikers and horseback riders. This particular one led to the camping area and cabin where her family used to vacation.

Still, Robyn wasn't quite up to the task, especially not after she read the writing below the arrow. *Area infrequently patrolled. Ski with a partner.*

She swung her head around and gave Karen a hard stare. "Are you crazy? I don't think I'm ready for that."

Karen laughed. "Come on. It's baby stuff. Not even backcountry. It'll be fun."

"What if I get hurt or stuck or—"

"You won't. But if you do, I'll send out the ski patrol," Karen said, with a waggle of her brows.

Visions of Sean rescuing her from a snowdrift and warming her up made her shiver, but with longing, not cold. Definitely not cold. "Okay, but I only want you to send one."

"Done," Karen agreed with a grin. And with that, she hucked off onto the trail rutted by recent skiers.

The wind blew a fierce gust of wind into Robyn's face as she stood there watching Karen take the run with confidence and ease. Could she do this? She'd wanted to take risks, to push her limits and test her boundaries, but she'd only just begun to enjoy skiing again, and she wasn't sure she wanted to make a total fool out of herself on a run she wasn't ready for.

On the other hand, she couldn't let Karen go by herself, and her friend was rapidly moving out of sight. Behind Robyn, the scrape of skis brought her head around, and some guy flew past, flashing her a bright smile. "Go for it!"

Ten years ago she'd have thought he was making fun of her or trying to get her to do something so she'd fail. But his gaze lingered on her a little too long, was a little too appreciative, and she realized he was encouraging her, was flirting, even.

She could do this.

Steeling herself, she pushed off into the considerably deeper powder, a charge of excitement sparking through her. Fat flakes fell on trees already drooping from the weight of the snow on their branches, creating a snow-globe landscape, a fantasy world where nothing could possibly go wrong.

Certain she'd made the right decision, she proceeded with slow, precise motions while she kept an eye on Karen's bright blue jacket ahead. Karen had slowed to give Robyn a chance to catch up, so she relaxed, enjoying the scenery and the silence, relishing the warming tingle of euphoria.

Then she rounded a bend and the trail opened before her, its steep slope and sharp drop-offs making her mouth go dry with the first glimmers of fear. *No.* She was an advanced skier capable of much more than she'd allowed herself to do before.

She picked her way down the trail, battling wind gusts that seemed to grow stronger by the second. Snow began to fall harder, creating a wall of white that decreased visibility and swallowed her friend.

"Karen!"

Karen's answering shout, distant but clear, brought her instant relief, and she spotted a glimpse of blue ahead. Karen had stopped to wait for her. Thank God.

Crouching, she took a leap from a ledge, and a blast of wind knocked her off balance. She hit the snow in a teeth-jarring impact. Her ski twisted, and she lurched forward into an ice-crusted drift. Pain shot through her wrist, and when she sat up she discovered an ugly red abrasion from snow-burn.

"'It's baby stuff. It'll be fun,' she says," Robyn muttered, struggling to her feet.

"Are you okay?" Though she was only a few yards away, Karen had to yell over the wind.

Robyn waved a gloved hand. "If that's the worst the chute can do to me, then bring it on!" Oh, yeah, that sounded brave, but she didn't think she'd take another one of these things anytime soon.

Snow began to fall harder, blown by winds that made it difficult for her to get back to her feet. No problem. They were at least halfway to the bottom now, and besides, every once in a while there were signs pointing to marked runs. They could always take one of those if they got into trouble.

She pushed off, choosing a conservative line and avoiding the more risky drops Karen favored. Karen veered off to leap from a ledge, and by the time Robyn skirted around the drop, her friend had disappeared into another wall of snow.

"Karen?"

No answer. She shouted again, hoping the wind had scoured out the thread of panic in her voice. This time she heard a faint noise that sounded like a distant yell, but she couldn't be sure. Fighting the wind and a growing sense of alarm, she headed toward a thick copse of trees where ski tracks crisscrossed, hoping one of them belonged to Karen.

Visibility rapidly decreased to the point where she couldn't see beyond a few feet, and fear became bone-numbing terror. She shouted Karen's name over and over, silently cursing her stupidity at agreeing to take the chute. She'd wanted to jump into life with both feet, but maybe she'd jumped into the deep end too soon. Time to admit defeat and head back to the groomed, well-marked ski runs.

She followed the tracks until they disappeared, swallowed by snow. Where were the marked runs? The blowing and falling snow had obscured her surroundings, and it occurred to her that she might be lost. Trying not to panic, she sucked in a deep breath and looked around. It took several seconds before she realized that the nearly frozen stream curving around twin boulders looked familiar. Her heart gave a kick of relief. If she was where she thought she was, she could ski to the camp area and find a cabin—the very cabin her father had bought.

The bad news was that the cabin was in the middle of nowhere, and in this weather she couldn't hope to ski out of here. Not tonight.

Disappointment and anger ripped through her at the realization that she wouldn't be meeting up with Sean at Après Ski, and their night together was ruined. So much for taking risks. It seemed that her personal life was doomed, because up to this point neither safety nor taking risks worked for her.

Teeth chattering, she pulled off her purple fleece scarf and tied it with clumsy gloved fingers to a tree branch, leaving a clue for anyone who came after her. The consequences of failure firmly in mind, she slid toward the cabin, hoping Karen had made it to the bottom safely and wondering how long it would take her to send out that search party.

"What did you say?" Sean froze in the middle of taking off his jacket. He stared at Karen, hoping he'd misheard. Someone bumped into him as he stood next to her table at Après Ski, but he barely noticed. "You lost her? On a Suicide Chute?"

Karen set down her mug of cocoa but kept her hands around the base, where they were so tightly clenched that her knuckles had gone white. "It's totally my fault. I wanted to prove she could do it. I thought it would be fun. She's a good skier. She'll be here soon."

Her words, spilled in a rushed jumble, rang hollow. Concern etched worry lines around her mouth and eyes.

"Have you checked your room? Other places she might have gone?"

Karen nodded. "I even left a voicemail on her phone. She

knows we're supposed to meet here, so I figured it would be the best place to wait."

He swore. Robyn was a good skier, perfect in form, but reserved. If she lost confidence in bad weather and on a poorly marked run, she could be in serious trouble. She could be lost, and without a radio or a GPS...

"Damn." He jammed his arms into his jacket.

"What are you doing?"

"I'm going to look for her."

He glanced at his watch. She wasn't technically missing, so he couldn't waste resources by calling out a search party, even if his inclination was to call out the entire National Guard. But he did need to hurry. Management had ordered several lifts to be shut down until conditions improved.

"I'm going to swipe a radio from the patrol office and tell the guys to keep an eye out. If she shows up, have someone call me."

He reached for the gloves he'd slapped down on the table when he'd come inside, and Karen grabbed his wrist. "She'll be okay, right?"

"Chances are that she skied a trail that took her to another part of the mountain and she can't get back until the lifts open up. She's probably hanging out in a warming house or village pub. If she's still out in the open, I'll find her."

He would. He knew the chute Robyn had taken, knew what areas were the most likely ones for skiers to stray when the trail grew indistinct in bad weather.

He left Karen wringing her hands, and after checking out a radio and informing the patrol director of his intentions, he caught the lift that would take him back to The Dark Side. His boss had wanted him to hold off until they could scrounge up a team to go with him, but all the teams were already busy, and Sean couldn't afford the delay. Not with the night closing in.

His stomach twisted in knot after knot as he exited the chair and skied to Chute Two off the marked run. The snow had gone from heavy to near-blizzard. He prayed Robyn had arrived safely back at the lodge and that he'd somehow missed her.

The deep, ungroomed snow presented a challenge, the blowing snow stung his cheeks, and the biting wind permeated even his thick clothing. He ignored it all. Robyn was his prime concern. Fear and adrenaline kept him warm and carving with aggressive functionality rather than finesse. He wouldn't win style points on this run.

Sticky snow left wet smears on his goggles, impairing his vision as he skied. He shouted frequently, slowing down in likely places for her to take shelter or be injured.

Nowhere. She was nowhere. He checked his radio to make sure it still worked and that no one had called to say she'd been found. The radio worked.

Where was she?

He hop-turned on an extreme steep and nearly went down. On the next turn, he did go down. Damn, this was getting tough. And if *he* was struggling...

He had to find her.

"Robyn!" The wind swallowed his shout. He barely heard it himself.

Then he saw it. Something purple and white fluttering at eye level a few feet away. He battled his way to the object, and when he reached out, his heart nearly froze. Robyn's scarf, so crusted with snow that if he'd passed by just a few minutes later, he'd never have seen it. Thank God. She'd been this way. But where did she go?

Quickly, he worked the knot loose and pulled it from the branch. He could picture the scarf as he'd seen it when they'd been skiing The Dark Side, wrapped around her warm, slender neck. A neck he'd throttle when he caught up with her. And when he was done throttling her he'd kiss that neck, her throat...everything he could reach with his lips.

He brought the scarf to his nose and inhaled deeply, taking in the faint scent that was uniquely Robyn. Welcome warmth oozed through his body, and damn if he wouldn't give his right arm to be holding her right now. But he wasn't getting anywhere by standing there.

He shoved the scarf in his pocket. There were several possible routes; one that would take her directly to the lodge, one that circled around the lodge and ended at a smaller ski area from which she'd have to catch a shuttle back, three that intersected with other runs, and one that led into the wilderness and some serious backcountry.

Since she hadn't yet been heard from, the last route was the most likely. It also happened to be the most dangerous and desolate. Why would she have gone that way?

Leaning into the wind, he struggled forward, wishing darkness would stop closing in. If he didn't locate Robyn soon, within the next half-hour or so, he'd be forced to take shelter in one of the hunting cabins that dotted the mountainside until he could get help from fellow patrollers.

Cabins. Of course. His brain must have frozen. If she'd come across a cabin, she could have decided to do the smart thing and stay. And if she was injured or suffering from hypothermia, she could be in serious trouble.

Swallowing to dislodge his heart that had jumped into his throat, he forced himself into high gear. He'd find Robyn or die trying.

Chapter Nine

Robyn closed her hand around the sturdy iron door handle, her heart pounding as hard in her chest as the person on the other side pounded on the door. She hesitated for the space of five or six spastic heartbeats, terrified of what she might find standing in the doorway. Would it be a rescuer, or some crazed nut case with an ax?

"Robyn! Are you in there? Open up!"

Sean! She tugged open the door. He stood there, pummeled by wind and snow, in the darkness broken only by the orange glow of the firelight flickering inside.

"Thank God," he said, his voice rough, as though it had been scraped over a sheet of sandpaper. "You scared the hell out of me."

"Ditto." She blew out a relieved breath. "But as you can see, I'm safe and sound."

He examined her intently, as if he was seeking injuries to prove her wrong, and then shifted his skis and poles to one hand and used the other to dig her scarf out of his pocket.

He held it out and said gruffly, "At least it wasn't your underwear."

At the reference to the bootie tree, laughter burst from her, even though the situation wasn't remotely funny, and if the grim set to his mouth was any indication, he didn't think it was amusing, either. Had something awful happened? She hugged her middle tight in a futile attempt to quell the alarm clawing at her gut. "Is Karen...?"

"She's fine. She sent me."

Relieved, she relaxed and stepped back, motioning him inside. "You must be freezing!"

He brought his ski equipment with him and removed his goggles and hat as he entered. "You think?"

The words had been casual, but the tone held an edge of...something. Anger? Worry? She helped him tug off his gloves and tossed them onto a weathered end table next to the prickly wicker thing that served as a couch. Other than the slightly labored sound of his breathing, Sean's silence hung heavy in the air. It was disconcerting to see the normally laid-back man at a loss for a joke or a smile, and she made an attempt to lighten the atmosphere inside the tiny cabin.

"Thank you for coming to rescue little ol' me."

He glanced around the cabin, his gaze pausing momentarily on the blazing fire in the hearth. "Looks like I'm a little late."

"You're surprised I'm not buried in a snowdrift?"

"Yeah, well, most of the women I know couldn't start a fire with a flamethrower and a pile of gasoline-soaked newspaper." He unbuckled his ice-crusted boots and stepped out of them. "What did you do? Rub two sticks together?"

She had to smile at how put out he seemed over not being able to play white knight. Poor baby.

"No." She swept up a box of matches from the dining table

to dangle in front of him. "But I could have. Girl Scouts." She shrugged. "Well, that and the fact that my dad used to drag us out camping with no gear other than what we could carry on our backs."

"And here I took you for an out-and-out city girl." He arched a tawny eyebrow. "You are full of surprises."

"And you're shivering." She helped him out of his jacket, shivering herself at the icy drops that fell onto her skin. "Let's warm you up."

He moved toward the fire, his stockinged feet barely making a sound. "Now should be the time I make some highly suggestive remark, but the part of my brain that thinks about sex is frozen."

"What's that leave, three or four cells that aren't frostbitten?"

He hunkered down in front of the hearth, no longer frowning but still not smiling. Tough audience. "Sounds about right."

"Let me get you some coffee."

"You made coffee?"

She pointed to the pot sitting on a rack over the fire. "Found that and some stale grounds in a cupboard. There's soup, too, if you're hungry."

Sean mumbled something that sounded suspiciously like, "Damon's an idiot."

"What did you say?"

He looked up from holding his hands before the leaping flames. "I said don't bother with it. I'm good."

"Yes, you are. I can't believe you found me."

Shrugging, he sat cross-legged on the bearskin rug she'd dug out of the bedroom chest and scooted so close to the hearth she felt sure he'd scorch himself. "I'm just glad you're okay."

"Of course I am."

"You're lucky."

At his stern expression, she huffed. "I would have made it back to the lodge if the blizzard hadn't started. And it wasn't like I went off into the wilderness without a plan."

"Just stick to the easy stuff from now on, will you? If you feel the need to push your limits, do it somewhere safer." He gave her another severe stare. "Promise?"

She rolled her eyes but nodded, knowing he was right. "Whatever. And FYI," she added grudgingly, "the mountain-cop routine is a serious turn on."

Amusement drew creases at the corners of his eyes, and finally, a quirky smile curved his mouth. "Good to know." He rubbed his hands briskly together and held them before the fire. "How did you get in here, anyway?"

"The cabin was unlocked. Mr. Delaney never locked it. Not much here to steal, and he always said he'd rather leave it open for anyone who might need to take shelter."

"You know the owner?"

"My dad just bought the place, but we used to come here a lot."

Now he looked even more put out than he had before. "So coming here wasn't an accident. You knew what you were doing."

She jammed her fists on her hips and gave a haughty sniff. "I might have lost my common sense for a crazy minute or two, but I'm not a complete idiot."

Chuckling, he unhooked his radio from his belt. "No, you are definitely not an idiot."

He keyed the radio, and after several attempts at speaking

through intense static, he finally made it clear to headquarters that they were safe and would be holed up for the night. He even told the person he spoke with to pass the word along to Karen.

It struck her then just how serious the situation could have been, how foolish she'd been to attempt a run she wasn't ready for.

"Thank you," she said when he finished. "I caused a lot of trouble, didn't I?"

"No trouble." He set the radio on the floor near the pile of split firewood. "But I could have thought of a better way to spend this evening."

She playfully nudged his knee with the ball of her foot. "A better way than what? Being trapped in a warm, candle-lit cabin with me?"

His smile...oh, dear God, his lovely, wicked smile made her knees weak and her breath hitch. "Well, now that you put it that way..." He bounded to his feet and grabbed her around the waist with astonishing quickness. "I can't think of anyplace I'd rather be."

The pounding of Robyn's heart when she'd answered the door couldn't compare to what was happening inside her chest right now. Sean hauled her against him, and the cold fabric of his clothes chilled her skin. She shivered, but it had nothing to do with the temperature.

Heat and a startling thread of tenderness swirled in his eyes as he brushed the backs of his fingers over her cheek. "I need to explain the other night."

She slid her hands up his stomach, her palms finding all the peaks and valleys of the six-pack abs beneath his thermal shirt. His chest expanded as she pushed her hands upward to wind her arms around his neck.

"Will the same thing happen tonight?"

Their eyes locked, and her heart stumbled. "Not a chance."

A surge of excitement raced through her, and her pulse hammered so hard it thundered in her ears. She pressed fully against him, letting him know just how pleased she was. "Then you don't need to explain."

"Yeah, I do—"

"Shh," she whispered, and leaned in to press her lips to his throat.

His breathing stilled, and somewhere deep inside he shuddered. His arms tightened around her, and when she looked up, his caramel eyes had darkened in the light cast by the fire and candles to a rich, pure amber that shimmered with desire. Slowly, too slowly, he dipped his head and took her mouth with the same forceful hunger she felt.

She sighed as the tip of his tongue teased her lips and then delved between them to meet hers. She tasted his need as much as felt it—electric, salty, tangy.

Melting against him, she dropped her arms to slip her hands beneath his shirt. Goosebumps pebbled his moist, warm skin and he shivered.

"You're freezing." She broke away and took his hand to lead him close to the fire. "Let's get you warmed up."

"I've got some ideas..."

"Me, too," she breathed, sinking to her knees on the plush bearskin rug.

She pulled him down in front of her and gathered the bottom of his shirt in her fists. The trip to the cabin must have been exhausting, but the rapid rise and fall of his chest now had nothing to do with exertion, a fact that thrilled her as she peeled the damp garment up over his torso and then tugged it over his head. His tousled hair stuck up all over the place, and she felt an intense urge to run her fingers through the spiky tufts. So she did.

Sean closed his eyes, let her comb through his soft hair. "That feels good," he murmured. "No one has ever touched me like that."

"Like what?"

His thick, long lashes swept up, revealing a tender intimacy that forced her to take a steadying breath. "Like they care."

The breath stuck in her throat. No no no! This was just sex. No caring or forming attachments allowed. Time to shift gears.

"Well, we can't have that, can we?" she teased. "Must concentrate on the lust." Smiling seductively, she trailed a finger down his temple, and along his cheekbone to his mouth, where she traced the bow of his upper lip.

"Lust is good."

He sucked the tip of her finger into his mouth and lightly nipped it with his teeth before soothing the spot with his tongue, and she nearly choked on the ball of said lust forming in her throat. Dragging her finger down, she skimmed his full lower lip, his chin, his neck to the hollow where his pulse pounded, and then lower, through the dusting of sandy hair covering the tan skin of his chest—skin marked with scars that read like a roadmap of pain. She examined each scar, wondering how they came about, and beneath them, sharply defined muscles rolled and flexed with the slightest touch of her finger.

"This one." She outlined a puckered, two-inch zigzag between his clavicle and left pec. "What happened?"

"Bad landing on a ski jump."

"Ouch." She kissed it, then dropped her hand down to a

thin, shiny line running between two ribs. "This one?"

"Collision with another skier."

"So many scars," she murmured, her fingers finding yet another. "So much pain…"

His hand covered hers, brought it up to his mouth, where he kissed her knuckles. "Sweetheart, you make me forget it all."

The cabin shrank and heated tension thickened the air like fog. Body pulsing with need, she lifted her shirt over her head, leaving her bare above the waist except for her bra—the green satin and lace bra she'd purchased today at a swanky shop near Hausfreunde, along with matching thong underwear. She'd wanted tonight to be perfect, had spent almost two hundred dollars she shouldn't be spending just so Sean would see her in the sexiest lingerie she could find. His reaction made the purchase worth every penny.

She could have sworn he stopped breathing.

His appreciative gaze took her in, and when he looked back into her eyes she knew she wouldn't have changed a thing about today. She would have spent the money on the lingerie, and she would have gotten lost and taken shelter in this cabin, because nothing else could possibly compare with the enchantment of the moment they shared right now.

In a lazy, fluid motion of ropey muscle, Sean pushed forward onto his hands and knees, his face mere inches from hers as she sat on one hip, her legs curled behind her. His lips, firm and warm, came down on her mouth. He eased her back onto the fur and stretched the hard length of his body against her. The kiss was tender, a caress, and it matched the gentle glide of his fingers up her waist, her ribs, her breasts.

A low moan escaped Robyn as he cupped her through the delicate fabric of her bra. His thumb swept over her hypersensitive nipple, sending swells of heat shimmering through her veins. Her own hands were idle, she realized. She'd been so thoroughly submerged in sensation that she'd become mindless with pleasure.

She ran her hands across his broad shoulders and over taut skin that stretched over the rippling contours of his back. His breathing came faster as she slowly slid them lower to the waistband of his ski pants, and when she brought her hand around to his pelvis and brushed against his erection, his breath hissed through his teeth.

"You're making me so hot I can't think."

She palmed his rigid length and flicked her tongue over his collarbone. "I don't want you to think. Just feel."

His naughty smile did the most wondrous things to her insides. "Oh, I feel." He eased her bra strap off of her shoulder and licked where the strap had been. "I want you naked," he whispered against her skin. "I want both of us naked."

Robyn had never wanted anything more. "Music to my ears. A Billboard hit."

She found the waistband of his wet ski pants and shoved them down his hips, only to be frustrated by the jeans he wore underneath. He helped, and moments later he was naked. Gloriously, deliciously naked, his skin bronze from the firelight, his body hard, honed, a work of art.

He pushed her back into the plush fur and leaned over her, eclipsing the firelight. Then he eased down her body to kiss her navel, his fingers working the zipper of her jeans. His kiss moved lower, to the hollow of her pelvis as he slid the jeans down, leaving her in only her skimpy satin thong and bra.

A familiar feeling of anxiousness twisted her gut. Why, oh why, could she not get naked with a guy without feeling like the fat teenager she used to be? She was in great physical shape; she knew that. So why did her old fears have to rear their ugly heads now of all times?

"You are so beautiful." He slid back up her body to nibble and nuzzle her throat.

"I-I have stretch marks..."

He pulled back, captured her gaze with his. "I have scars."

Robyn melted. The look in his eyes, the one she'd craved all her life, one of honesty and worship and wanting, made her soften inside.

But this was supposed to be a fun sex-fest and nothing more.

Gathering her wits, she pasted on a flirty smile as she reached down to take his velvety erection in her hand. "You're not so bad yourself, you know?"

Air whistled through his clenched teeth as he sucked in a breath. "You have no idea how good that feels."

She stroked down the impressive length and then back up to run her thumb over the plum-ripe head. "Tell me."

She felt his groan all the way to her gut. "Like warm silk and, ah, yes..." He bit his bottom lip and closed his eyes.

Thrilled to bring him such mind-bending pleasure, she slid her hand down farther, to the soft skin of his balls. His eyes snapped open and he grabbed her hand with a breathy, "No."

A bead of anxiety bubbled up in her throat. Was he going to back off again? She couldn't take another rejection. "Sean?"

"Shh, baby," he murmured with a smile that seemed a little shaky but that dispelled her concern nevertheless. "Nothing's wrong. It's just that what you're doing feels so damned great that I'm about to lose it." He drove a finger into the leg opening of her underwear, his knuckle grazing her clit and making her gasp as he worked his way back down her body to tug them off. "Can't have that yet."

With a flick of the wrist, he tossed her expensive thong across the room like it was nothing but a dust rag, and then he circled her ankles with his hands as he knelt between them. She felt exposed and vulnerable—and aroused beyond anything she could ever have imagined. Desire had coiled so tight inside her that when he slid his palms along her calves, her womb contracted with the beginnings of a release she already knew would take her apart, physically, emotionally and every other way a person could shatter.

His hands massaged their way to her thighs and she shuddered when his thumbs stroked the crease where her legs met her sex. Butterfly strokes caressed inward until he slipped a finger between her folds and brought her hips right off the bearskin rug.

"You're so wet," he said gruffly, and she whimpered.

She wiggled, aching for his touch. He smiled, knowing exactly what she wanted, but he drew out the torture by stroking everything but her pulsing clit. His fingertip circled her slick entrance, over and over, then he gently pinched her folds between his fingers, the pressure at once a relief and a torment.

Finally he flicked his thumb over her swollen, ultra-sensitive knot of nerves as a finger pushed inside her. She cried out, and again her hips arched upward to meet his touch. Her body was on fire, her skin burning, and she knew she was going to die from the intensity of what he was doing with his hands.

"Tell me what you want." His hot breath fanned across her inner thighs, and she nearly jumped out of her skin.

"That." She writhed, squirmed against his hand, needing his touch in exactly the right place. "Right there. That's what I want."

Another finger joined the first, pressing deep, and his thumb circled her center, starting wide, but working inward until she was panting, unable to take in enough air.

"Sean," she gasped, "stop, or else—"

"Or else what?" He grinned and dipped his head between her legs to replace his hands with his tongue.

Robyn bit down on a cry of pleasure as his tongue swirled and plunged inside her in a rhythm that sent her thoughts careening into orbit. She gripped the bearskin beneath her until she thought clumps of fur would tear loose, and she couldn't keep her hips from lifting to meet Sean's talented mouth.

"You taste good," he whispered in a voice rough with the need he controlled in order to bring her pleasure. "Like summer rain."

That was it. All she could take. She welcomed the fiery tug of approaching orgasm, the sweet, spiraling sensation that whirled faster and faster as heat from the fire lapped at her skin and Sean lapped at her sex.

Release captured her and she couldn't contain the scream of ecstasy as her climax took her, hard and deep. She hadn't even settled her hips back on the floor when Sean covered her, his mouth on hers, his muscular body so welcome against her.

He took her mouth hungrily, nipping lightly at her lips and sucking on her tongue, mimicking what he'd done to her sex. The sensation brought her back to the height of arousal.

Still kissing her, he fumbled for his jeans and withdrew a condom from his pocket. Thank God he'd brought one, but disappointment came quickly on the heels of relief.

"You always so prepared?"

Rearing back on his knees between hers, he shook his head. "No, but when you called..." In the flickering light from the fire, she saw him blush as he rolled on the condom. "I was hoping."

She wanted to believe him, that he didn't always carry around rubbers in the event that some hot groupie propositioned him, but she wasn't stupid. Still, his admission that he'd been hoping to use it with her made her shiver with pleasure.

Then he was on top of her and she couldn't think anymore, not with the way his erection was stroking her slick opening but not pushing inside, the way desire pooled and pulsed through her entire body.

He teased her, and though she marveled at his control, she didn't want it. Not now. Later, maybe, but now all she could think about was the way her inner muscles would stretch and clench around him. She lifted her legs, captured his waist between her thighs, and arched against him, desperate to feel him inside her.

"Greedy thing," he growled, sliding his cock through her swollen folds, and she nodded, too far gone with lust to speak.

Finally he entered her, his thick shaft filling her with molten heat. He thrust home with a low groan, then ground slowly against her until that fierce need crackled and popped at the tip of each nerve ending.

Reaching up, she twined her fingers through his hair, pulling him closer with her hands and her legs, unable to get enough of him. He cupped a breast in his palm and drew the nipple into his mouth, nibbling and suckling, stroking it with his tongue. When he lifted his mouth away, she cried out in frustration until he kissed a path to her ear, where he told her how perfect she was, how sexy, how much more he wanted to do to her.

The downy softness of the bearskin rug beneath her contrasted with the steel hardness of the man above her, and she loved it. Loved the opposing sensations that assaulted her on the inside as well as the out.

He thrust faster, and his hot, panting breaths whispered over her ear and neck, sending tingles zipping across her skin. He looked at her then, his whiskey-gold eyes glittering darkly, and instantly she shattered, and then he shattered, too, calling out her name.

Arms shaking, he collapsed on top her, his weight more welcome than she'd ever have guessed.

"Baby," he breathed, "you're amazing."

She'd never been called amazing before, but neither had she believed a man could be as amazing in bed, or on rug, as Sean was. How often did that happen, two people finding a chemistry between them that was so combustive it threatened to burn them up?

And she absolutely didn't want to think about how rare what they'd found was, because that would lead to all kinds of trouble.

So though it took a long time before she could speak, she managed a polite and generic, "You're not so bad yourself."

Chapter Ten

It took an eternity or two for Sean's breathing to return to normal, and even longer for his body to stop pulsing from the aftershocks of what Robyn had done to him. Not that he was complaining. Sex with Robyn had been incredible, a life-giving blast of oxygen, and if he spent the rest of his life huffing like he'd just skied a slalom, he'd be perfectly happy.

Gazing up at the log rafters, he absently trailed his knuckles along the gentle curve of her upper arm as she lay next to him, her head nestled in the crook of his shoulder. She snuggled closer and pressed a tender kiss to his throat. Unbelievably, desire stirred in his loins once more.

How the hell had that idiot, Damon, let her go? How had any man not seen what Sean saw—the caring, fun-loving, self-assured woman who managed to blend city girl savvy with small-town sensibility? Yes, she'd taken too big a risk by tearing up a slope too advanced for her confidence level, but her error in judgment was something he could understand—the need to push one's limits in order to feel alive, to prove that life was more than simply existing in a daily grind. He could count on one finger the number of women he'd dated who could start a fire with two sticks and prepare coffee in the hearth.

And that one finger was Robyn.

Maybe Damon couldn't deal with the fact that a part of her seemed inaccessible, just beyond reach. That side of her personality drove Sean nuts because he wanted all of her, not just the scraps she doled out.

He frowned, watching the shadows from the fire dance on the ceiling. No, self-absorbed Damon didn't seem like the type of guy who'd even realize Robyn kept part of herself detached and concealed. Secret.

And truth be told, a couple of years ago Sean wouldn't have noticed, either. Two years ago, Sean Trenton came first in all things. Number one.

God, what an ass he'd been.

But now that his ego had been stripped down to its essence, he could see deeper than the surface. And he wanted more than anything to ferret out what lurked beneath Robyn's surface. He wanted to learn her secret.

But maybe he first needed to let someone in to see his own secrets. He'd taken his first step toward the cure for his insecurity by making love to Robyn. Now he needed to take the next step. The last step.

His gut churned at the thought of baring his soul to ridicule or disgust, but then Robyn nibbled at his earlobe, and his anxiety melted away like a late spring snow on a warm day.

"Mmm, it's been forever since anyone has done that to me. Feels great."

"Yeah, right." She underscored her disbelief with a nip on his lobe that stopped just short of pain.

"What? It does feel great."

"Not that. The forever part. You probably have women lined up with tickets."

"The Sean ride?" He snorted. "Shut down due to

maintenance problems. No longer exists."

"Oh," she began in a throaty, seductive voice, "I assure you, it exists. And in perfect working order."

When he chuckled, she propped herself up on an elbow and busied herself by raking her fingers through his chest hair. "All right then, I'll bite. What's your idea of a long time? A couple of weeks? A month?"

"You're going to think I'm a freak," he warned.

Her hand stilled on his chest, and she gave him a sincere, solemn look, belied by her playful tone. "Sean. Baby. You're afraid of clowns and cornfields. I already think you're a freak."

He grunted. "Clowns are scary. Admit it."

Gazing at his chest, she resumed her play, drawing a series of figure eights on his sternum. "You're avoiding the question."

"Yeah, yeah." He hesitated, listened to the fire crackle and pop. Oh, what the hell. "I haven't been with a woman in two years."

A disbelieving smile quirked her mouth. "Funny. Now, seriously. How long?"

"Twenty-four months." And one week, two days, and some odd hours.

Her smile faded and her hand froze once more. "Oh my God, you *are* serious."

"As a heart attack."

She must have sensed that they'd crossed into new territory, treacherous territory, because she swallowed and stared into the fire for a moment before asking the question he knew would come. "Why?"

It would be so easy to make something up, to avoid this, but he'd run from it long enough, and for a man who had never run from anything in his life, running felt like losing. And losing felt like hell.

"I told you I had an accident two years ago, right?" To his dismay, his voice broke, but she seemed not to notice, only gave a slow, single nod and cocked her head to the side so the razor-cut ends of her silky hair brushed his arm and chest.

"There was more to it than that. A lot more." Her hand started moving over his chest again, this time in long, soothing strokes over his heart. His heart that had gone tachy from anxiety.

"It's okay if you don't want to tell me," she murmured.

He laced his fingers behind his head, exposing himself totally to her, something he hadn't done for anyone but doctors since his surgery.

"I want to tell you. See, my accident wasn't exactly an accident. I was angry, reckless, and skiing stupid." Stupid hardly covered it. Barely scratched the surface. He'd been hell-bent upon outrunning his problems, and if he killed himself while trying, so much the better. Problems solved.

"I took a header off a ledge and slammed into a boulder. Broke my leg and a few ribs." He laughed, and the bitter sound echoed off the log walls. "Made doubly sure my Olympic hopes were dashed forever."

"What do you mean by 'doubly'?"

Blowing out a long breath, he sat up, pulled the wool blanket from the couch, and settled it over her shoulders. He remained sitting, propped against the couch, and she stretched out, draping herself across his lap, one breast resting on his thigh. She cupped her head in one hand, facing him as he faced the fire.

"Six weeks before I was supposed to ski in the Olympics, I was diagnosed with testicular cancer."

"Oh. Oh, God. I'm so sorry."

He shrugged. "It's okay. I survived, I'm over it."

"Then why is it so difficult to talk about?" She pushed up slightly and studied his face. "Ah. You haven't told anyone."

Damn, she was sharp. "No one but family. And Todd."

Todd, who made teenagers look mature but who'd been a loyal friend since childhood. They'd learned to ski together, and when Sean's talent left Todd behind, he'd become a strong patroller and a great paramedic.

"Why not?"

He wrapped a thick lock of her hair around his forefinger and stroked it with his thumb. "At the time I didn't need a pity party or a media circus. I let everyone except my family and friends think the accident was what kept me from skiing."

"And now?"

"Now? Now I just feel like a freak."

She sat up, curling her legs against his and holding the blanket loosely around her shoulders, a questioning look in her eyes. "You feel like a freak because you had cancer?"

"No, I feel like a freak because—" He couldn't say it. Yes, he could. Just spit it out. "Because I lost a testicle."

He could still hear his father's military-honed, football-coach voice pinging off the inside of his skull. *"Get it together, son. I won't accept anything less than perfection! You ain't perfect, you ain't nothin'!"*

Sean had grown up under the former drill sergeant's inflexible thumb, had been raised to believe that in any aspect of life, from sports to relationships, if you weren't perfect, you were a failure. His dad had been puffed up with pride at his only son's accomplishments—until the diagnosis that forced Sean to withdraw from the US Ski Team in order to undergo life-saving surgery and radiation treatments.

For some reason, his father had taken the entire situation as a personal affront, as if Sean had intentionally contracted cancer just to annoy him. *"You let me down, boy. Our shot at gold is gone, and how are you going to have a kid now to pass on your ability? Gone forever."*

Logically Sean knew his dad's words were meaningless; it wasn't his fault he'd gotten cancer, and doctors had since assured him that he could most likely still father children, but years of having the idea of perfection drilled into his head had messed with his self-esteem.

"Sean?"

He blinked, realizing he'd been somewhere much less pleasant than where he was right now with Robyn. "Sorry. I drifted."

Lips pressed together, her expression thoughtful, she looked down into the puddle of blanket in her lap. "Did you consider an implant? They have those, don't they?"

Nodding, he reached out and rubbed his palm over her knee. "I had one. My body rejected it a couple of months later, and I was back to being a freak."

"Look," she began softly, "I can't know what it feels like to lose what you did, but I do know how it feels to be self-conscious about your body. You aren't a freak, and I can't imagine that anyone would think that."

"Yeah, someone did."

Jenny. The first woman with whom he'd tried to overcome his anxiety after the surgery. He'd pushed past his fear like he always had, managing to mask his nervousness even when she'd touched him intimately.

Then she'd discovered his defect. She'd recoiled. She'd tried to cover up her reaction, telling him she'd merely been startled. But he'd seen her look of disgust. He'd zipped up and walked out of her hotel room, never looking back, but her expression had haunted him ever since.

Robyn's hands formed fists around the handfuls of blanket, and possessive anger ignited in her eyes, so intense he almost smiled. "Someone actually called you a freak?"

"She said it was freaky."

The anger faded, and color returned to her knuckles. "Freaky. Is that all she said? Was she insulting?"

"That wasn't insulting enough?"

"I'm sure it seemed that way at the time."

He sputtered at that. "*At the time?*"

"Sean, listen. Trust me on this." She reached out to take his hand, and it was all he could do not to jerk it away. "She wasn't making fun of you. You were feeling exposed. Hypersensitive. I know. I've made the same mistakes."

"Yeah, I'm sure you're an expert in losing a nut."

She winced, stung, and he regretted his show of temper, his sullen remark she didn't deserve. "I can't relate to that, but I can relate to being self-conscious and scared." She bit her bottom lip, torturing it until he thought it would bleed, and then she blurted, "I used to be really fat and ugly."

Only the expression on her face, the very real pain etched into the creases on her brow, stayed his skeptical laughter—or his furious curse. He'd dated women who'd sworn an extra pound meant obesity, that a few freckles rendered them fit for the kennels. Robyn hadn't struck him as one of them, and even now, while he couldn't believe she'd ever been overweight and ugly, he saw that she believed it.

"Go on," he urged, giving her hand an encouraging squeeze.

"I was so paranoid that if I overheard someone saying anything that might be even remotely construed as rude, I flipped out. Once, I overheard someone say the word 'cow' and I started crying. Turned out they were talking about a farm project."

She brought his hand up to her lips, where she pressed a gentle kiss into his palm. "My point is that what you took as an insult might not have been. In any case"—she gave him a long, appraising look—"you have nothing, I repeat *nothing*, to be worried about."

Desire slammed into him. Man, pathetic what two years of celibacy and a heated gaze from a beautiful woman could do to a guy. "Given the predatory look on your face, I'm thinking I *do* have something to worry about."

A wanton smile touched her lips, and she stretched with a slow, feline grace, causing the blanket to slip off her shoulders and pool around her perfect, plump bottom. While he tried to catch his breath, she spread his legs and kneeled between them, her hands on his knees. Still smiling and looking into his eyes with a smoky gaze, she ran her hands up his thighs until she reached his hips. Blood pounded in his ears, nearly drowning out the sound of his raspy breathing.

She traced a pattern of who-cared-what over the tight muscles of his abdomen, her hand occasionally brushing his rock-hard erection. Each time, he nearly jumped right out of his skin, and each time, her smile widened.

"Still worried?" She circled the tip of one finger around the swollen head of his cock.

"More than ever," he choked out.

Need swirled in his belly, spinning faster and faster with each teasing stroke of her finger. Then her hand went lower, delved between his legs. He stiffened, grabbed her wrist and drew it away.

Her gaze softened, brimmed with emotion and understanding. "Please. Trust me."

The hand holding her wrist shook no matter how hard he tried to control the spastic trembling. She was asking so much of him, too much, and nothing, not even the time he'd been caught in an avalanche, had terrified him as considerably as what she wanted him to do.

He swore as if harsh words could chase away the mind-numbing terror, and then, taking a deep breath, he released her. Surprisingly, she didn't move her hand from where he'd lifted it to his thigh. Instead, she bent forward and kissed his navel, her soft lips bringing him back to the place where fear was not welcome.

Her breasts brushed his thighs as her silky hair brushed his now straining erection, and sparks of electricity charged through his bloodstream. She kissed a path lower, letting her cheek caress what her hair had only teased. A sweet, feathery sensation skated over his skin, and he had to concentrate on keeping his thoughts rational.

She grasped his shaft, stroked lightly. Her hand moved lower, and a moan caught in his throat. Lower. He resisted the urge to push her away. Lower, and her fingers found what they sought, and he went rigid, his hands clenched so tightly they hurt.

Robyn didn't stop kissing his abdomen as she fondled him, and when she took the head of his penis between her wet lips, he almost forgot what her hand was doing there between his legs.

"You taste good, Sean," she whispered in a sultry voice that nearly made him lose it right then and there, "and you feel good."

She gave his testicle a gentle squeeze for emphasis, and sharp bursts of pleasure speared through him. And then she put her mouth *there,* kissing and blowing warm caresses that brought his hips off the floor.

He unclenched his fists and drove his fingers into her hair, holding on for dear life as she sucked his sac into her mouth, laved it with her tongue. Her fingertips stroked the tender strip of skin behind his scrotum, each pass sending shocks of pleasure through his flesh and into every cell until the sensation centered in his swollen cock.

He moaned as she licked a trail back up, along the seam of his shaft to the head, where a drop of precome had formed. The warm, wet heat of her mouth had him writhing, his thighs shaking as she lapped up the creamy bead. She continued to taste him, dragging the flat of her tongue up his abdomen to his chest, his neck, and finally, as she settled her opening over him, his lips.

"Got another condom?" She swiped his bottom lip with her tongue as she hovered above him.

"Shit. No."

"I'm on the pill...haven't been with anyone since my last checkup..."

He gripped her waist, dying to pull her down and bury himself in that hot, sweet place between her thighs. "I'm clean. It's been two years and my job requires testing every six months—"

He didn't have a chance to finish before, eyes closed, she kissed him with hungry, punishing kisses and guided him inside her slippery sex. He wished he knew what emotions lurked behind those delicate eyelids, but as her warmth and slick passage surrounded him, he let his curiosity go, hoping only that she could feel what she meant to him.

Bracing her hands on his shoulders, she raised and lowered her hips, sometimes deliciously fast and furious, sometimes so agonizingly slow that she barely moved. He let her set the pace, but twice he had to crunch his teeth together to the point of pain in order to keep completion at bay.

The wicker couch bit into his back, but he welcomed the discomfort, used it as a focus when clenching his teeth or biting his tongue started to fail. Robyn wrenched her lips away from his and sat back on his thighs, her eyes open now and glazed with fierce desire. Her hair, well mussed by his fingers, glowed by the light of fire. Man, he'd never seen anything so wild, so sexy, so perfectly made for him.

He lifted his hands from her rocking hips to her breasts, stroking them, eliciting gasps from her when he lightly pinched her tight, hard nipples. The flickering firelight cast deep shadows between her breasts and made the sprinkling of freckles across the swells more prominent, made it more tempting for him to want to count every single one, to know her so thoroughly that he'd be aware the moment a new one appeared.

"I love the sounds you make," he said raggedly. "You are so hot. And tight. Sweetheart, you're killing me."

She smiled and threw her head back, closing her eyes and increasing her pace. Unable to take more of her torture, he dropped a hand to her mound and slipped a thumb into her cleft, finding the sweet bundle of nerves he'd loved with his mouth earlier. She bucked, clenching around him, and the game was over.

She came loudly, grinding against him and forcing his own fantastic, powerful release. He grasped her hips and drove upward as the orgasm ripped through him. Red flashes burst behind his eyes, and he felt a rush he never thought to experience anyplace but on skis. Jesus, what this woman did him was a one of a kind microbrew experience compared to the cheap, mass-produced quality of past pleasures.

Completely and thoroughly spent, his body trembling, he pulled her to him and wrapped his arms around her.

"So," she purred, "was that so bad?"

He would have laughed if he'd had the energy or breath. "Baby, I'm cured."

Chapter Eleven

The smell of pancakes infiltrated Robyn's dreams. She came awake to the blurry sight of Sean flipping a burned pancake in a cast-iron skillet over the fire. He shot her a grin over his shoulder.

"Morning. Found some paper plates and flapjack mix in a cabinet. I hope you're hungry, and I mean *hungry*, because you'll need to be starving to eat these things."

The bear fur tickled her skin as she stretched and quickly tucked her arms back under the warm blanket they'd slept beneath. The cabin had a bedroom with two bunk beds and a cot, but with no electricity, they'd have frozen if they hadn't slept in the room with the fireplace. Besides, this way they could sleep together.

"Believe me," she said on a yawn, "they can't be nearly as bad as the stuff my dad used to make us eat on camping trips."

"Uh-huh. You haven't tasted these bad boys yet. Emphasis on bad."

She laughed and blinked away the sleep in her eyes so she could better take in the man crouched on his heels before the fire in his jeans and snug shirt. No way would she ever tire of looking at him. Or touching him. Or making love—no, *having sex* with him.

Love. Not even close. She had no business pairing that word with what she and Sean had, which amounted to a fling with great sex. Out-of-this-world great sex.

But there had also been an intensely emotional connection in what they'd done last night. She'd shared intimate details of her past with him—she never told any man how overweight she'd been—and he'd confided a secret so deep and personal that the risk he'd taken pierced her soul.

His confession hadn't shocked her, but it had blown a hole in her defenses. Two years. He'd gone two *years* without sex because the loss of a testicle had ravaged his self-esteem. And for some reason, he'd decided to bring her into his tight circle of those who knew the true reason for both his celibacy and his withdrawal from the world of competitive skiing.

He'd wanted for her to be the one with whom he tried to push past his feelings of inadequacy. But why her? And now that he was "cured", as he claimed, what was to stop him from taking up with hot groupies and willing divorcees again?

She burrowed deeper into the blanket, unsure if she truly wanted to know the answers to her questions. She had too much going on in her life right now to have to deal with Sean's motivations. And even if she didn't have job and reunion issues...oh, *crap*.

Levering into a sitting position, she glanced frantically around the room for a clock. She didn't care that the blanket slipped down to her waist, exposing her breasts to the chilly air.

"Sean! What time is it?"

He slid two pancakes from the pan onto two paper plates and glanced at his watch. "Eleven-oh-six."

"Oh, no." She scrambled to her feet, ignoring the cold and hurriedly grabbing up her clothes, which were scattered all over the cabin. "I have to go. I have to get to a phone." She stepped into her thong, thankful that the flimsy fabric had withstood Sean's enthusiasm. Where was her bra?

"Ahem." He still crouched there by the fire, the plates at his feet, his grin cocky and his finger twirling said bra. "Looking for this?"

Glaring, she snatched it from him. "Hurry up. We have to go."

He shook his head and held out a plate and a bottle of what looked like ancient maple syrup. "We aren't going anywhere. Not until the storm passes. I even called patrol, and they can't help us get out of here until there's a break in the weather."

She stepped into her jeans and grabbed her ski pants. "We can't wait for your buddies. I have to make a call before noon or I lose a job and an auction emcee."

He cursed, finally realizing the seriousness of her predicament. "Robyn, we can't get out. It isn't that we shouldn't. We *can't*."

Her heart gave a giant thump and her stomach knotted. "Of course we can. We just ski out of here—"

"It's too dangerous. By the time the storm is done, we may even need help to dig out."

Refusing to believe him, she rushed to the door and yanked it open, only to find a wall of snow four feet high, and above that, a white veil of blowing snow trying to fight its way in. A few lumps fell inside and broke apart over her bare feet. Her stunned brain barely registered the stinging cold.

Oh, no. Oh, God, no. This couldn't be happening. Maybe they could climb up and over...

She attacked the snow, shoved her hands into the solid pack in an attempt to scoop handfuls aside. She'd dig out with her fingernails if she had to.

"Robyn." Strong arms closed around her from behind. "Baby, stop."

She ignored him, continued to drag chunks of snow down onto her feet. Pain shot up her arms and her fingers burned, but she didn't care. She had to get to a phone.

Sean's arms tightened, steel bands around her as he dragged her away from the door. "You're hurting yourself."

"No!" She struggled uselessly against him, cursing the warmth of tears on her cheeks. "We can get out. We can!"

Even as she spoke, she knew he was right, but stopping meant giving up, and giving up meant losing everything she'd hoped for.

"No, we can't." His voice, low and gentle against her ear, didn't soothe her, but it did convince her she was acting like a crazy woman.

Sniffling, she turned into his embrace and clung to him like he was her entire world. Which, as they stood in a musty cabin in the middle of a forest, he was.

"I'm so screwed," she mumbled into his shirt. "What am I going to do?"

"We'll handle it."

His words rumbled deep in his chest, and she felt them against her cheek and in her heart. Great. How was she supposed to stay detached when he said things like that? Things that made her think he liked her for who she was rather than how she looked? Why did he have to be so wonderful?

"No, *we* won't handle it. I will." She wheeled out of his arms and dashed away the moisture in her eyes. "I always do."

He shut the door and walked back to her, leaving wet footprints on the floor from the dusting of snow that had blown through the doorway. "What if I can help?"

"You can't."

"But what if I could?"

Stubborn man. "You *can't.*"

She spotted the pancakes where he'd placed them on the table before dragging her away from her panicked attempt to tunnel out of the cabin. Shivering from the cold she'd let in, she plopped down in one of the rickety chairs. She wasn't hungry, but she needed a distraction. And an excuse not to look at Sean.

"I know people. I could make some calls."

"I don't want anyone hiring me as a favor." She grabbed a fork out of the package of plasticware he'd set out at some point. "I'm good at my job and I'll find another one based on that." She took a bite of pancake. "Also," she said with a grimace, "don't ever open a breakfast restaurant."

He laughed. "That bad?"

"That bad." But she took another bite. Anything to keep from thinking about her latest disaster. Besides, a girl had to keep her strength up around a sex machine like Sean.

He sat down at the table with his own plate and drenched his pancakes with syrup. "So what now? Do you have more job options?"

"You seem really concerned about my work situation."

Shrugging, he cut up his pancakes with his plastic fork. It took effort, she noticed. "I hate to see you upset. I want to help."

Part of her wanted to hug him for being so sweet, and part of her wanted to slap him for making her want to hug him. "Stop that."

"Stop what?"

"Being wonderful. Trying to fix my problems." She shifted in her seat and steeled herself for what needed to be said. "I don't think getting involved any deeper in my life is wise."

His fork halted halfway to his mouth. "Why not?"

"Because there's no point." She shoved to her feet and tossed her plate of half-eaten pancakes in the kitchen wastebasket. "I'm going to be gone in a week."

"So?"

"So...this is fun. But that's all. Let's not take this thing we have any deeper or someone is going to get hurt." That someone being her.

He put down his fork and pushed his plate away. Something that looked like pain flashed in his eyes, but it must have been a trick of the firelight because no way could Sean believe what had gone on between them was more than sex despite the closeness they'd shared. They'd talked about this at the warming house, discussed jumping into a fling with both feet. Changing the rules now would be unfair.

"What is this thing we have?" he asked softly.

"We have sex."

"Great sex," he amended.

"Better than great sex."

Sean gave a single nod and dragged his gaze slowly down her body, and then even more slowly back up, and the atmosphere in the cabin suddenly thickened as the air charged with electricity. When his eyes finally captured hers, the hunger in them made her shiver, only this time, the cold draft was in no way responsible.

"But is that all we have?" One corner of his mouth turned up in a sexy half-smile. "I mean, not that insanely mind-blowing sex is anything to sneeze at."

"No, it's not. But I'm sure you've had lots of mind-blowing sex. I'm one more name on your list."

He'd glanced down at something on the floor, but now his head snapped up. "Robyn—"

"Please, Sean, isn't the sex enough? For now, at least?"

She kicked herself for adding that last, the part where it sounded like maybe they could eventually have more. Who was she trying to make feel better? Him? Or her?

It didn't matter. She knew it wasn't right to judge him on his past—the women, the fame, the money, and neither was it fair to assume that if all that came back to him he'd change. But she knew what fame and fortune did to people. She'd been around enough radio personalities and pop stars to know. And she wanted none of it, ever again.

Her relationship with Sean could be about only one thing. And she'd prove it.

Stepping closer to him but just out of reach, she peeled off her turtleneck and flung it to the couch. Then, under his narrowed gaze, she unhooked her bra. Slowly, so slowly she could barely stand it herself, she eased the straps down her arms and sent the bra skidding across the floor to his bare feet. He sprawled back in his chair, legs spread wide, his pose deceptively relaxed, but the flare of his nostrils and the tic in his jaw gave him away.

Smiling, she unzipped her jeans and stepped out of them, loving how his fists had clenched over his thighs and how his Adam's apple bobbed with every hard swallow. His reaction was a drug that chased away even the tiniest threat of anxiety and filled her with a confidence she'd never experienced. Boldly, she smoothed her hands from her throat to her breasts, where she cupped them, caressed the nipples with her thumbs until they tightened into sensitive peaks.

"I'm imagining that my hands are yours," she said, as she slid them to her waist and hooked her fingers on the elastic waist of her thong. Keeping an eye on her audience, she tugged down the already damp scrap of material.

A gruff sound escaped Sean when she turned slightly and bent over, and she took her sweet time rolling her spine straight again. She stood there, amazed at her utter lack of self-consciousness. He stared at her like she was a goddess. Never had she felt so powerful and attractive.

"Do that again," he ground out. "Bend over."

Heart pounding in anticipation, she turned toward the fire and bent forward, bracing one hand on the back of the wicker couch and placing the other between her legs, high on her inner thigh. She could hear Sean's deep, rapid breaths grow raspy as she drew her hand upward and slipped two fingers into her wet slit.

Sean made a strangled sound when she inched her legs even farther apart and spread her lips wide. "So." She tossed her head to look at him from over her shoulder. "Are you just going to sit there, or do I have to take care of myself?"

✳ ✳ ✳

Only a fool would have turned down what Robyn offered, and Sean sure as hell wasn't a fool. He'd shoved to his feet with such force that his chair had slammed back against the wall, dropped to his knees behind her and punished her with his mouth for teasing him. He fucked her with his tongue until she begged for him to do the same with his cock. He could still hear the slap of his thighs against the back of hers as he took her from behind in a raw, powerful joining that had wrung them both dry and left them in a state of pleasant exhaustion.

He smiled as he wrenched himself away from Robyn's sleeping form and sat up on the bearskin rug. He skimmed a finger over the soft skin of her hip, knowing exactly how she tasted there, so sweet and warm.

She was sweet, all right. And stubborn as a damn mule.

Why didn't she want his help finding a job? Who would turn that down? Irritation tugged at him, but he suspected that some of it came from the fact that if she didn't want something as minor as his help, she'd be furious about the deal he'd made with Damon.

And why did she want their relationship to be about nothing but sex? He'd tried to bring up the subject several times throughout the day, but each time she distracted him. Pleasantly, but still.

He'd been under the impression that she wanted more, that when she'd said she wanted to jump in with both feet, she meant a real relationship. But all along she'd been talking about mindless sex. All along, she'd wanted what all the women of his past had wanted—either instant marriage to a celebrity and the lifestyle that came with it, or, as in Robyn's case, a shallow fling with the stereotypical athlete who went for quantity, not quality, when it came to women.

Shaking his head to clear his mind of the troubling thoughts—thoughts that he *had* been the stereotypical athlete, he pushed to his feet and fed the fire with one of the last logs stacked near the hearth. If they weren't rescued soon, they'd be in trouble. He shot a look at the wicker furniture, though, and figured they'd be doing Robyn's dad a favor by burning it.

His stomach rumbled, and he glanced at his watch. Almost five o'clock. They'd taken a break between bouts of lovemaking to share a can of chili, but that had been three hours ago, and he was starving. Hopefully the storm had died down and they could ski out of here to some real food.

Quietly, he donned his clothes and opened the door. Snow

had piled in the doorway, leaving only a foot or so of clear space at the top, but through the narrow opening he could see blue sky. Finally, they could get out. He shut the door and used the radio to call the ski patrol. Rick, the supervisor, said he'd already sent Shane and Curtis on snowmobiles to check on them.

Sure enough, the moment he unkeyed the radio, the faint rumble of engines joined the snapping of the fire. He turned to wake Robyn, but she must have heard him talking with Rick and had already scrambled up to dress. What a shame. She looked great naked.

"What time is it?" she asked.

He didn't want to tell her. The reunion party he was supposed to take her to had already started in the lodge's ballroom. "Time to get out of here." She gave him a no-nonsense stare, and he sighed. "Five-thirty."

Running her fingers through her tangled hair, she frowned. "Great. I was supposed to meet up with the other charity event coordinator at five to discuss the auction on Saturday."

"We shouldn't be that late. The guys will have us out of here in no time."

"By the time we get back to the lodge and clean up, she'll probably have left."

He reached for his jacket. "We can still try."

"Are you always so optimistic?"

"Are you always so pessimistic?"

"Yes. See why we wouldn't make a good couple?"

He shrugged. "Opposites attract. We make a great couple."

"We aren't a couple," she said with a sniff.

Impossible woman. The hum of the snowmobile engines grew louder, and he zipped up his jacket. "We'll talk about this

174

later."

"No, we won't. There's nothing to discuss. This is a fling, Sean. Nothing more."

Karma had a cruel sense of humor, because how often had he said those exact words in the past? "If I wasn't who I am, could it be more?"

She looked away. "I don't know."

So he'd been right; this was still about his fame and fortune, even though he'd tried to convince her none of it made a difference. He wasn't going to be a famous athlete again. And the sports announcer thing...well, that could be a one-time shot. He might hate it. He might be terrible at it. One thing was for certain though; he sure as hell wasn't going to tell her about it now. Knowing her, she'd cut off even their physical relationship if she knew.

He moved to the door to put on his boots, and she followed him to lay a hand on his arm. "You're okay with this just being a fling, right?"

"Yeah. I can deal with it."

He could. After all, a fling had been what he'd wanted from the beginning. The point of meeting Robyn in the first place had been to get laid so his life could get back to normal, which meant success and lots of women begging at his feet.

That sounded great. Too bad it didn't sound nearly as great as it had a few days ago.

✻ ✻ ✻

It took just under an hour for Sean's ski patrol buddies to dig them out and give them a lift to the lodge on the snowmobiles. Robyn spent another hour showering, changing and pinning her hair up in a loose chignon. Now, she and Sean strolled along the lodge's convention center halls toward the ballroom where the reunion party was well underway. Music popular during the years Robyn had been in high school grew louder.

And the knot in her stomach grew larger.

She pressed a clammy hand to her belly to steady her nerves as they threaded their way through a group of people talking outside the towering double doors, probably to escape the noise inside. No one recognized her, which hardly came as a surprise, but several people cast double takes at Sean and whispered his name.

"I can't believe you made it home and all the way back so fast," she said as they entered the huge anteroom plastered with blown-up pictures taken from her class yearbook. "Aren't the roads a mess after the storm?"

He shook his head. "The north side of the mountain took the brunt of the frontal system. Road crews have already cleaned up the southeast side." His gaze took a slow ride down her body, taking in the slinky black knee-length dress she'd slipped into. "You look great. I've never seen a woman look so good in heels in my life. Have I told you that?"

"Once or twice," she said with a laugh, "but keep it coming."

"How about if I keep you coming?"

"You are very, very bad, Sean Trenton."

His naughty wink sent pleasant shivers straight to her core as they paused at the doorway to the foyer. Inside, two women sat at a table scattered with nametags.

"Well," Sean began, "are we going to go in, or do you want to do something more...fun?"

She gave him what she'd intended to be a sideways glance, but he looked so good in a blue dress shirt, tie and black slacks that she couldn't help but stare for a lot longer than qualified as a glance.

"And I suppose you have something in mind?"

"I have a lot of somethings in mind."

Oh, but she adored this man. "C'mon. Let's at least take a look around so I can say I was here. And I need to see if Linda is around, let her know how the auction plans are coming along."

Or how they *weren't* coming along. She could only imagine how enjoyable it was going to be to admit that she would be emceeing the auction instead of a celebrity as planned. She'd spoken with Linda, the assistant coordinator, two days ago, promising results, but now it didn't look like she'd get a replacement for Damon. She'd even called the local radio and television stations to see if a resident personality could volunteer, but everyone was already booked for events related to the ski and snowboard competitions.

Sean stopped her before they could take a step inside. "You're really stressed about the auction. I know it's a big job to coordinate everything, but why is it so important to you?"

She could hear Karen's voice echo in her head. *You don't need to prove anything.* But she did. Maybe not so much to the people of her past, but to herself. Maybe, if she could face her demons, she'd scale back her insane drive to get to the top. One of her main hopes for a successful reunion and auction was that she'd feel better about herself, would be secure enough with her own measure of personal success to be content with a job in a smaller, more relaxed media market. Seattle or Portland, maybe, where she wouldn't feel the pressure to be someone she wasn't. Where she might enjoy the job again.

"Robyn?"

"It's not that important," she lied, partly because now wasn't the time or place to have this discussion, and partly because she hardly wanted to admit the truth to herself, let alone Sean.

He eyed her skeptically. "This is about what you told me in the cabin, isn't it? It's about how these people treated you in high school."

She said nothing, but understanding dawned in his eyes. Nodding sharply, as though he'd made a decision, he squeezed her hand. "I'm with you, baby. Let's go."

Robyn felt as though her heart would burst through the walls of her chest. She wanted to kiss him, but instead she squeezed his hand back, hoping he understood how grateful she was, how much his strength meant to her.

They stepped into the foyer, and she instantly recognized Rochelle Saxony, who had always been pleasant, if frosty. The other woman, Janice Hunter, had been an obnoxiously smart beauty whose jealousy of Robyn's academic achievements had resulted in some of the cruelest torments in school. She and Gigi had been best friends.

"Can we help you?" Janice asked, all smiles. "Are you a graduate from our class?"

"I'm Robyn Montgomery."

No doubt Gigi had warned them ahead of time that Robyn the Troll wasn't fat and ugly anymore, but the forewarning apparently hadn't been enough, because their eyes almost bugged out of their heads.

Rochelle found her voice first. "Gigi said you looked great, but..." Her gaze flickered to Sean and back. "Wow."

Janice held her hand out to Sean, who let go of Robyn's

and grasped Janice's with a firm shake. "And this must be Sean Trenton, about whom I've heard so much." She released him with obvious reluctance and flashed him a blinding smile. "Would you like to see what your date looked like back in the day?"

No! "Thanks, Janice, but we're in a hurry. Is Linda Brandenburg still inside?"

"Oh, she left. So there's no need to rush off," Janice said with a dismissive wave. "Besides, it's fun to reminisce, isn't it?"

She whipped open the senior annual, and Robyn's stomach bottomed out. She'd confided to Sean that she'd been unattractive, but she hadn't told him *how* unattractive.

Gigi and two other women who had been part of the "in" crowd in high school chose that moment to appear, and Robyn prayed her advanced-formula deodorant lived up to its promises, because she was starting to sweat.

"You're just in time," Janice announced, a wicked smile twisting her cranberry-colored lips. "We're looking up old pictures of Robyn."

"Oh, fun!" Gigi chirped. "There's a good one on page eighty-three."

Janice flipped to the page Gigi had mentioned and then, with glee in her eyes, spun it around to Sean. Robyn felt ill. There she was, posing for the school newspaper staff photo. She'd been at her heaviest ever, her complexion had been a disaster and her thick glasses had only added to the horror.

Rochelle gave Robyn an apologetic look and reached for the book. "That's enough. Let's go get some food."

Janice pulled the yearbook from Rochelle's grasp and looked up at Sean as though the other woman hadn't spoken. "Amazing, isn't it?" She tapped the picture with a jeweled nail.

Until now, Sean's expression had been closed, unreadable and utterly unlike him. At Janice's snarky question, he smiled thinly and reached for Robyn's hand.

"Yeah, it's amazing," he said, and Janice and Gigi exchanged looks of mutual satisfaction. "Amazing that ten years later, you still act like you're in high school."

He slammed the book shut and turned to Robyn, fierce anger and possessiveness lighting his eyes. "Stay or go?"

Her chest grew tight around her somersaulting heart. Sean surprised her on every level, and as she stood there with his hand in hers, she felt every one of her defenses crumble. It felt good. Scary, but good.

"Go." She slanted him a grateful smile. Then she turned to the gaggle of red-faced women and realized that she, too, was still acting like she was in high school. She'd given them way too much power over her, and it had to end. "And to think, I was in a hurry to get here, when I could have spent more time alone in a cabin with him. What was I thinking?"

Slinging his arm around her, he shook his head with theatrical sadness. "I tried to tell you that, but you wouldn't listen," he said in a voice meant to be overheard. "Good thing I just happen to have a cabin where we can be alone again."

"Mmm, I can't wait." She really couldn't, which startled her as much as anything else had tonight. "But you know, I think I'd like to at least get in one dance."

"Anything you want. *Anything.*"

She wouldn't have traded that moment for the world. The moment where her ex-classmates went from crimson-faced with shame to green with jealousy. The moment where Sean looked at her like she was the only woman in the world.

The moment where she realized that while the scars of her past would always be with her, they would never again define her.

The glittering ballroom looked like something straight out of a fairytale. Crystal chandeliers sparkled from the high, open-beamed ceiling, a champagne fountain flowed at the back of the room where tables loaded with food lined the walls. Candlelit tables seated with former classmates and their dates and spouses lined the sidewalls, and in the very center, the dance floor teemed with couples moving to a classic love ballad.

As they stepped onto the dance floor, Robyn was grateful for both the crowd and the slow song, since she'd never been able to dance to anything with a fast beat, and the crowd would keep her from standing out.

Though with a man like Sean at her side, they wouldn't not stand out for long.

"So," he said into her ear as she wrapped her arms around his neck and began a slow, languid sway against him, "why the dance? Why not get out of here?"

"Believe me, I'd love to go. But I never attended any of the school dances. Not one. I've always felt like I was missing something because of it." She cast a glance back at the entrance to the ballroom, where Gigi and Janice stood watching. "And this time, no one is chasing me away."

Moving to the music's rhythm, she tilted her head back to peer into his handsome face and gorgeous golden eyes, eyes that grew heavy-lidded as she rocked her body into his. "Besides, we're here, so I might as well show you off."

At the small of her back, where his fingers had been massaging the skin bared by the low-backed dress's design, his hands stilled. "Might as well. Wouldn't want to waste the date, right?"

"Did I say something wrong?"

A smile played on his lips. "No. I just want you to have a good time."

His arms tightened around her, and she snuggled close, breathing in his clean, male scent as he led her around the floor, his steps fluid and sure. "Just one dance, and then I want to be alone."

"Like I said, anything you want. This is your night."

It was on the tip of her tongue to tell him to stop it, to quit saying wonderful things like that, but she didn't want him to stop. She wanted him to keep being wonderful and to keep telling her what she needed to hear. To keep looking at her in that way he did, like he was doing right now with that gaze that was more of a caress.

"Robyn...what are you thinking right now?"

She looked around the elegant room at the people watching them from their tables and realized she should have been nervous, minding every step, every move. Instead, she was relaxed, enjoying herself, even.

"I'm thinking that these past few days have been amazing. And it's all been because of you."

Dipping his head, he slid his cheek against hers. "I was thinking the same thing. I can't remember ever feeling this way with a woman."

Pleasure speared her. Panic should have. But tonight was too perfect to worry about why his words should have bothered her, and instead, she just accepted that she was growing more and more comfortable with him.

"Can I ask you a question?"

"Sure, babe."

She drew in a deep breath and looked up at him. "Have you ever been serious with a woman?"

"Never." He spun her in a circle that took away the breath she'd drawn. "But I need to be honest with you. I've dated a lot of women."

"How many is 'a lot'?"

"More than I'm proud of."

Some warped part of her wanted to ask for a number, but the other parts knew she might not like what she heard. "Never even a little serious?"

He shook his head. "I didn't go into relationships looking for anything permanent." His hand splayed wide against her back, and he pressed her close, wrapping her in his warmth. "But you aren't just another name on my list, Robyn. I want you to know that."

"I do know that," she said quietly, marveling that despite what she'd said to him at her father's cabin, she believed him. She didn't want to, but she did.

The tip of his finger trailed up and down her spine in gentle, soothing strokes. "What about you? Anything serious in your past?"

This was something she never talked about except with Karen, but after sharing her fat and ugly story with Sean, she'd reached a level of ease with him that surprised her and left no hesitation when it came to revealing her past. "The thing with Damon was the most serious relationship I've ever been in. Which is pathetic, since it was more off than on in the two years we dated."

Her entire dating history, in fact, was pathetic. She finally lost her weight—and her virginity—her senior year of college, and she spent a couple of years making up for lost time. It had been fun, at first. She'd traded up men like she traded up radio station jobs.

Then she'd gotten the position of a lifetime at KFAB. Six

months later, she and Damon were dating. Six months after that, they broke up for the first time because he "needed space". It didn't take long for "space" to dump him and move to Paris, and he'd convinced Robyn he wouldn't need "space" again. From that point on, their relationship remained steady but casual, until he got the job at the television station. Things fell apart quickly, and just before she could give Damon the boot, he'd done it. On a Post-It note. Stuck to her office chair.

"It's not pathetic," Sean said. "At least you tried. I've never made it more than three months."

"Yeah, I tried." For what reason, she had no idea. She'd allowed Damon to walk all over her, to treat her like nothing more than a prop at parties and an outlet for sex. But she'd also come to realize that she'd encouraged his treatment by keeping her emotions to herself, for giving him absolutely no reason to love her.

She'd learned her lesson. She'd opened up to Sean, and had been rewarded with a deep connection that was both frightening and thrilling. And although she still wasn't sure how this fling would play out, she was beginning to think that no matter what, the positives would outweigh any negatives.

"Sean?" She pressed fully against him so her belly encountered the hard length of his cock. "Let's go home."

"You think we can make it all the way there?" he teased, as he nipped at her earlobe.

She groaned. "I just hope we can make it to the car."

Chapter Twelve

The shrill clang of the alarm clock woke Sean way too early, especially given that Robyn hadn't allowed him to get to sleep until well after midnight. The memory of what they'd done into the wee hours of the morning stirred his cock and made him smile. If she wanted to use her fine body to keep him awake for a month straight, that was okay with him.

Smothering a yawn, he rolled out of the spooning position in which they'd slept and hit the snooze button. When he turned over again, he found Robyn on her back, looking at him through heavy-lidded eyes. Norbert, who'd slept in his usual spot curled up behind Sean's knees, meowed and jumped off the bed, annoyed by the activity.

"Hi," she said in a raspy morning voice that sent his blood rushing south.

"Hi."

Sunlight spilled through the slatted wooden blinds on the window, falling across her freckled shoulders in streaks of light, setting fire to her hair that splayed out over the pillow. The dark green flannel sheet covered the gentle swell of her breasts, clinging to her curves. She looked good in his bed, but he'd known she would from the moment he laid eyes on her.

"You have to work today?" She rubbed her eyes.

"Unfortunately."

She wriggled onto her side and dragged a fingernail inch by slow inch from his wrist to his shoulder. "Unfortunately? I thought you liked your job."

"I like being with you more."

A sleepy grin tipped the corners of her mouth. She sat up, pushed him onto his back with palms pressed to his pecs. "You always say the right things." She nuzzled his neck, nipped lightly at his collarbone as her fingers threaded through his chest hair.

Desire shuddered through him as she threw a leg over his thighs, straddling his waist and cushioning his erection against the soft curls of her sex. He smoothed his fingers along her curved calves and then up her thighs to the firm flesh of her hips. Grasping her waist, he lifted her and settled her back down, sheathing himself inside her warm opening.

"You're so beautiful." He reached up with one hand to stroke her cheek.

She closed her eyes and rubbed against his palm like a contented cat, the sheer ecstasy of touching and being touched evident in her expression. He'd never been with a woman who enjoyed him like she did, who seemed to crave his innocent caresses as well as his sexual ones.

And their mutual enjoyment had grown since the reunion thing last night. He'd been shocked by the high school picture he'd seen, but he'd been even more stunned by the behavior of her classmates. No wonder she'd been so supportive about his cancer. He'd suffered the effects of a crushed self-esteem for a short two years; she'd suffered her entire life.

It broke his heart that his outraged reaction, something so minor, had affected Robyn so deeply that she'd transformed before his eyes there in front of her old tormentors. The wall she'd kept carefully between them had crumbled, leaving behind a woman who'd started to open up during the dance, and who'd laid herself bare to him later at his cabin, sharing everything about her childhood, her adult life, her love life.

His hopes for a real relationship with her had soared, and even though they hadn't talked about it, he felt sure something permanent was now a possibility.

Even the sex between them had changed. He hadn't believed it could get better, but the spark had intensified, and every time they made love, he left more of himself with her. It was exhilarating.

And daunting.

Never had he invested so much emotion in a relationship outside his family—his father had taught him that love was conditional. But now it was time to gamble.

As if she'd heard his thoughts, she opened her eyes and watched him, her gaze so noticeably free of the glint of misgivings that had always been there that his breath caught. She hadn't said it, not verbally, but she'd told him with her actions that this wasn't playtime anymore. She probably hadn't even admitted it to herself yet, but she would. She had to. He'd never been a good loser.

He thrust his hips up, drove into her with the force of what he felt for her, and her eyes widened in surprise before they went smoky green, like a forest on fire. She nuzzled his palm and captured his index finger between her soft lips. Drawing his finger inside her mouth, she stroked the pad with her tongue. A moan dredged up from somewhere deep in his chest.

Her moist heat circled his finger and his shaft. Though her body remained perfectly still, he nearly lost it right then and there.

"Robyn. Baby, you're going to get left behind in a second here," he said raggedly.

She released his finger and angled forward to brace her hands on his shoulders. "Don't worry. I'll catch up."

Biting her lower lip in the way she did when she concentrated, she lifted and lowered her hips in an agonizingly slow rocking motion. He knew she didn't need help, but in about two seconds he was going to be useless, so he dropped a hand between their bodies, dragged his thumb through her folds to the swollen bundle of nerves in the center.

He stroked her as he thrust upward, and she cried out, shuddered in her release. He went over the edge with her, his spasms intensified by hers. God, he loved how she did that, how she clenched him with her internal muscles and at the same time clenched him with her hands like she didn't want him to go anywhere. That wasn't going to happen.

Gathering his arms around her, he pulled her to him for his kiss, holding her close as their bodies came down from the high of sexual release. The alarm sounded again, reminding him that he needed to get up, but it felt too good to be with Robyn. He could spend all day in bed with her.

For the first time ever, he wanted to hang out with a woman instead of carving up the slopes. Before the cancer and accident, sex had been an extravagant way to kill time when he couldn't be on skis. He'd enjoyed women and the pleasure that came with having one naked, but he'd never chosen sex over skiing.

Now he'd gladly give up his day on the slopes to spend it with Robyn. Todd would think he'd lost his mind, would accuse him of being pussy whipped, and truth be told, Sean would have said the same thing a couple of years ago. But something had changed, and it was a change he liked.

He kissed Robyn's throat, feeling her pulse pound against his lips. "I have to get up, sweetheart."

She sighed and rolled off him. "Probably a good thing. You're going to wear me out."

"Me? Wear *you* out?" Snorting, he climbed out of bed and pulled on pair of shorts. "Somehow, I doubt that."

She propped herself up on an elbow. "Are you implying that I'm a nympho?"

"You say that like it's a bad thing." He winked, and she laughed. "Help yourself to whatever you want in the kitchen. I gotta clean up."

He showered quickly, and when he stepped out of the steamy bathroom, it was to the smell of coffee. Not wanting to waste a moment of time with Robyn, he hurriedly dressed and went downstairs, where she sat at the kitchen table wearing a pair of his boxers and a T-shirt.

The intimacy of her body clad in his clothes got his libido charging again. Damn, she'd done a number on him.

When she saw him, she looked up from the old ski magazine she'd been reading. "I hope you don't mind me digging through your drawers for something to wear."

He stopped behind her chair and brushed his lips across the back of her neck. "You can dig through my drawers anytime," he murmured.

She snorted, and he could almost hear her rolling her eyes. "Men."

Chuckling, he grabbed a travel mug from a cupboard and filled it with coffee, hoping the brew was as strong as it looked.

"Oh, wow." Robyn's wonder-filled voice made him grin as he turned.

"Yes, my ass is nice, but I doubt that it's worthy of such awe," he quipped.

She gave him a "you're hopeless" look and pointed to a

page in the magazine. "You do have an ass worthy of awe, but in this case, it's this ass."

He walked over to the table and peered at the picture, which turned out to be a photo of him on skis in mid-air. "Yep, awe-inspiring."

When she looked back up, she fairly glowed with joy, which put big blips on his trouble radar. She didn't like reminders of his past life. She should have been sulking, not smiling.

"This article, it's about you."

"Well, it's about the ski team..."

She flipped the page. "And here you are on the set of Oprah."

"Okay, that part is about me..."

She pointed to another page, her movements animated and excited. "You're signing autographs!"

Yeah, something was definitely off about this. He leaned down and looked her in the eye. "Are you okay? Do I need to get my medic kit?"

Laughing, she shut the magazine. "I'm great! Better than great. I just realized that what I've been looking for is right under my nose."

He took a sip of coffee, wishing it contained a shot of whiskey, because he had a feeling he was going to need it in a second. "I'm not following."

"Well, you know how you said you wanted to help me with my job? I think I've found a way for you to help."

"Does it involve sex?" he asked hopefully.

Grinning, she stood and padded to the coffeemaker, where she topped off her mug and turned around to prop a hip against the counter. "No, and it's not my job, exactly, but you can still help."

Not one shot of whiskey. Two. Or three. "Okay."

Biting her lip, she looked down at her feet as though trying to get up the guts to speak. "The charity auction is tomorrow, and I still don't have an emcee." She peered up at him through thick lashes, a hopeful spark in her eyes. "You'd be perfect. Can you do it? Please?"

Damn and double damn. He'd love to help, and the auction thing even sounded fun. But he couldn't get out of announcing the ski competition if he wanted to. God, he couldn't even look her in the face.

"Robyn...I'm sorry. I can't. I have to work."

"Oh." The devastation in her voice nearly killed him. Guilt settled in the pit of his stomach as she moved back to the table and plopped back down in the chair. "I know I shouldn't ask, but can't you get out of work? Can someone take your shift?"

What could he say to that? Yes, he could get someone to cover his shift if he were patrolling, but he wasn't. He could tell her the truth, but now wasn't the time, not when he needed to get to work and when she was already upset.

A few days ago, the fact that he didn't tell her about the announcing job seemed like a simple omission—granted, an omission designed to get her into bed, but still, it had been innocent enough. But then he fell for her, and now it felt like a lie. A big lie.

An unforgivable lie that doubled in size every day he kept it secret.

Worse, he'd bungled badly when he agreed to keep her busy in order to secure a permanent sports-announcing job. Even if she forgave him for the first lie, she'd never forgive the second betrayal. And he wouldn't blame her. In his blind desperation to get his old life back—the life of fame, fortune and women—he'd not considered how his selfishness would impact others. Others like Robyn.

He'd thought the deal with Damon would benefit her, but deep down, had he really been more concerned with helping himself? Probably. Idiot.

"Sean? Can you do that? Get someone to work for you?"

The hope in her words stabbed at his heart. He couldn't help her with the auction, but he was going to make things right. This wasn't the fling she kept insisting it was. This was real, and he was going to be honest with her about everything. But first he had someone to deal with.

"I can't," he said as he threw on his coat. "But don't make plans tonight. We need to talk, and there are some things you need to know. How about if I meet you in the Moosehead after work?"

She nodded and he leaned over to kiss her. "I'll see you later."

Trying to contain her disappointment, Robyn watched Sean walk out the door. *Damn!* She'd been so sure she'd solved her problem. What people from her high school class thought about her was no longer the main issue; this was about the charity and Sean would have brought in a lot of money.

And what did he want with her tonight? He'd sounded serious, like whatever he wanted to say wouldn't be all sunshine and flowers. Emotions warred with each other, some wanting the discussion to be about creating something more permanent between them, and others—weaker, traitorous ones—wanting the discussion to center on cooling things down.

Oh, God, what if he *did* want to pull back? What if the new intimacy they'd found together last night had been too much for him? What if he'd given some thought to that picture of her in the yearbook and had decided that the risk of her letting herself go again was too much? What if he was right now rehearsing the "it's not you, it's me" speech?

A panicky, fluttery sensation filled her chest as "what ifs" filled her mind. Then Karen's lecture at BrewSki just days ago rang in her head. *You get freaked out and start inventing worst-case scenarios before you get all the facts.*

She did do that. She was doing that now. Sean had given her absolutely no reason to think he'd dump her, and the fact that she worried about it opened her eyes. Why was she fighting what they had? His past was the past. He was a simple EMT and ski patroller now. He didn't want any kind of sports comeback. He said he was done with groupies, and the fact that he was now fully functional but hadn't ditched her for a hard-bodied bimbo in a tight snowsuit was proof of that. So what was her problem?

She sipped her coffee and sat back in the chair to think. Well, the long-distance relationship thing could be an issue. She didn't know where she'd be working—if she could even get a job—but she knew she couldn't get anything closer than Denver, which was hours away.

Then there was...nothing. So really, other than distance, nothing would prevent them from having a real relationship.

Assuming, of course, that Sean wanted a relationship. Maybe she'd read him wrong. She'd never been the best judge of men. If so, she'd have seen through Damon a long time ago.

Norbert rubbed against her foot, and she reached down to scratch behind his ears. "You're daddy's quite the guy, isn't he?"

Norbert blinked his luminous eyes at her, but she knew he'd agree if he could talk. Sean had saved his life, something a lot of men wouldn't have done. That alone was worth giving him a chance at something more than a fling.

A sense of relief and elation washed over her at the decision, and feeling giddy, she bounced up the stairs to shower. When she finished, she put on the jeans and sweatshirt she'd changed into after the dance. She'd followed Sean in her rental, which had given her the freedom this morning to go to the bakery while he worked.

Once dressed, she headed downstairs to call Karen for a lunch date. The phone on the little table next to the staircase rang before she could dial, and the answering machine picked up.

"Hey, Sean, it's Samantha," said the nasally female voice. "I have fabulous news. You ready? Sit down, because I booked you on Letterman next week! Can you believe it? I also contacted all the sports magazines and TV channels to let them know you're back on the scene. Two already want interviews."

She paused, which gave Robyn a chance to breathe, something she'd stopped doing at the word "Letterman".

"This is a good thing, Sean. Trust me. This'll lead somewhere big. Oh, and good luck with the announcing tomorrow. Just give the camera your signature smile, and the world will fall in love with you all over again."

The lady, who must have been his agent, hung up, leaving Robyn shaking with rage and barely able to suck a breath through her constricted windpipe.

Sean lied.

The pain of betrayal shredded her insides, and her eyes stung with tears he didn't deserve. What a lying, cheating rat!

She whirled away from the phone, determined not to dissolve into tears. Not here, where competition medals and trophies mocked her for falling for Sean's lines. Hands shaking, she grabbed her purse and coat and flew out of the house. Bright sunlight glinted off deep snow, but she couldn't take pleasure in the splendor of a winter morning. She needed to get away from him, away from his house. The most comforting place she knew was only a few miles down the mountain, and amidst the delicious aroma of baking bread and sweet pastries, she could drown herself in food.

Chapter Thirteen

The warble of an ambulance's siren competed with the sound of Sean's panting breaths in his ears. Sweat streamed down his spine beneath his patrol jacket, but his hands had nearly frozen in the cold air as he crunched a series of compressions into a heart attack victim's chest. The man had collapsed in the lodge's parking lot while loading his ski gear into his van, and Sean and Todd, who'd been on their way to the patrol office for a change of shift, had been closest to the scene.

"Paramedics just turned into the lot," Todd said from his position at the older man's head.

Sean nodded, counting out his thrusts. The grate of cracked ribs beneath the heel of his palm shivered up his arms with each downward stroke. The siren cut off as the rumble of an engine grew louder.

He stopped after the last compression and waited for Todd to ventilate the patient with breaths through a mask over the man's nose and mouth, and then his partner pressed two fingers to the man's neck.

"Got a pulse!" Todd removed the mask and bent close to the victim's face and gave a relieved smile. "He's breathing. Holy shit, he's breathing."

"Thank God." Heart attack victims rarely came back, and though the patient still had an uphill struggle ahead, at least he stood a better chance of recovering now than he had a few minutes ago when he was turning blue in the snow.

The paramedics, employees at the same company for which Todd and Sean both worked, took over, and after they loaded up the patient and the crowd of bystanders dispersed, Sean and Todd started back to the office to fill out paperwork.

"Man, that was awesome." Todd grinned and held up his open palm.

Sean slapped his friend's hand and stuck his frozen one back in his pocket. "Definitely a high."

It had been a long time since he'd done more than patch up serious but non-life-threatening injuries, and he'd forgotten how good it felt to save a life. How it gave him a sense of purpose and accomplishment not even his championship medals had.

The late afternoon sun cast long shadows as it sank behind the mountain, and skiers fresh off the runs swarmed inside the lodge for food breaks. Sean had to wade through the masses until he and Todd finally made it to the patrol office, where they finished up paperwork and changed into civilian clothing. Todd took off, late for his EMT shift.

Sean prepared for battle.

Allowing himself a grim smile, he mounted the lodge stairs to Damon Slade's room. He'd waited all day for this, had anticipated the coming confrontation to the point of distraction—distraction that resulted in two idiotic falls even a beginning skier would have had to work at to achieve.

Although, Damon hadn't been the only distraction during a busy day on the slopes. The competition had him stressed to the limit. He hadn't spoken publicly in years. What if he made a complete fool of himself?

He mulled that over for a moment. Why hadn't he cared about making a fool of himself back in his pro skiing days when he'd regularly said stupid things to reporters? Probably because he'd been immature and shallow as a mud puddle.

He topped the landing on the second floor and cast a glance in the direction of Robyn's room. Robyn, who had been his other distraction today. Robyn, who had kept him up until all hours of the night.

His grim smile became genuine. Somehow he had to convince her that they were meant to be together in more than a sexual way. He loved being with her, loved talking to her. Loved her. No use in denying it.

He took the next flight of stairs two at a time. On the third floor, he found Slade's door, and knocked. Through the thick wood, he heard muffled giggles, a curse, and then approaching footsteps. Damon opened the door wearing only sweat shorts.

"Mr. Trenton. What can I do for you?"

Behind the other man, a nude blonde dashed to the bathroom. Sean basked in smug contentment. Robyn was his, and Damon was stuck with a woman who couldn't possibly compare.

"I need to talk to you." Sean shot a meaningful glance over Damon's shoulder. "Alone."

Damon's eyes narrowed slightly, but he nodded. "Let me throw on a shirt." He retreated into the room, and returned wearing a radio station sweatshirt. Stepping outside, he pulled the door closed behind him. "What's this about?"

Anxious to wipe the patronizing smile off the other man's face, Sean let him have it. "Deal's off. I won't keep Robyn busy for you anymore. I'm done."

He'd keep Robyn busy, but not for anyone but himself. The whole arrangement hung over him like a dark cloud, and he wanted that cloud gone. She deserved better.

A tic pulsed in Damon's jaw. "What happened? What did she tell you?"

"She hasn't said anything about you." Nothing Damon needed to hear, anyway.

"Then what's the problem?" His face paled. "You didn't tell her about our arrangement, did you?"

Interesting that Damon seemed so worried. Why was it so important that Robyn didn't know about their deal? What was at stake? All questions Sean hadn't thought of when Damon had first approached him to keep Robyn away from him. It hadn't mattered.

Now it did.

"I'm curious," Sean said. "Why do you care if I told her?"

"Mr. Trenton, I don't owe you any answers. All I owe you is a shot at building a career. And right now that shot is a little shaky."

Right on cue. After what Damon had done to Robyn, Sean had expected this.

"About that. Here's the thing." He shifted slightly closer to Damon, wanting to enjoy every trace of emotion that played over the other man's face. "Thanks to the contract we both signed, I'm announcing the ski competition tomorrow no matter what. If I'm good, you'll hire me even without my having to entertain your ex-girlfriend. If you don't hire me, someone else will. It's that simple."

"I see." Damon patted the breast of his shirt as if searching for something. Cigarettes, probably. He smelled like a dirty ashtray.

"And what about Robyn?" Damon's eyes darkened, sharpened into shark-like beads. "What about her job?"

"She'll figure something out." And he'd help her as best as he could, whether or not she liked it.

"Are you sure about that?"

Damon's softly uttered question struck a warning chord inside Sean, and when the other man glanced over Sean's shoulder, his stomach took a deep dive. He knew before he looked that Robyn stood behind him. Damn. And damn again. How much had she heard? Judging by Damon's cool smirk, she'd heard enough.

The pounding of his heart threatened to crack his ribs. Feeling sick, he turned. Robyn stood at the top of the stairs, her face ashen, her eyes burning green fire.

"Karen said she saw you come up here," she croaked. "I needed to talk to you, so I followed, and...and...bastards!" She spun around and fled down the stairs.

"Robyn!"

She didn't stop, or even slow down. Cursing, Sean followed. A swarm of skiers in the lobby swallowed her, and his insides clenched on a panicky sensation. Where'd she go? He stood on the bottom step and scanned the crowd. She was nowhere.

Shouldering his way through the throng, he crossed to the Moose to see if she'd ducked inside, but again, she was nowhere. She must have gone outside. He burst through the lodge doors, and there, fleeing toward the parking lot, was a fox-red head of hair illuminated by light from the Victorian-style sidewalk lamps and the strings of bright white party lights in the village.

He ran as fast as his snow boots would allow, and as he closed the distance between them, he wondered if the emotional distance would be so easily bridged.

Robyn's breath scorched her throat, and even the icy air she sucked in great gulps did nothing to ease the burn. She'd been angry enough after listening to Sean's agent and learning the truth about his bogus I'm-done-being-famous crap. But to discover that he'd been scheming with Damon in order to land a job...what an *asshole*.

Heavy, snow-crunching footsteps sounded behind her. "Robyn. Stop. Please."

She increased her pace.

"Let me explain."

She halted so suddenly that her foot slipped on the hard-packed snow and she nearly went down, which made her even angrier, and she whirled around with a snarl.

"Explain? Explain what? That you used me? That you lied to me to get me into bed? That you conspired with a man you knew I detested so you could get *a job*?"

He had the grace to blush. "Yes. That would be what I need to explain."

"Why? So I'll sleep with you again? Fat chance, sport. Go feed someone else your lies. I guarantee it'll take a lot less work to get another woman into bed than it will be to get me there. Because it won't happen. Ever."

Clenching her fists so she wouldn't be tempted to strangle him, she spun around and stalked toward the parking lot. His raw curse followed her, echoing crisply in the mountain air until the too-merry pub music from a bar in the village ate it up.

"Robyn, I don't want to get you into bed."

Stung, she stopped, faced him once more. "Why? Because you only slept with me to keep me busy for Damon? Was having sex with me that much of a sacrifice?"

He studied his boots, perhaps unable to look her in the eye, and her stomach rolled at the possibility that her remark had been on target.

"You were a sacrifice," he admitted in a tight voice, "but not in the way you think."

"Really."

A group of people carrying skis over their shoulders walked past and Sean stepped forward, taking her hand before she could stop him.

"Let's talk somewhere quiet."

He started to lead her back to the lodge, but she tore away from him and jammed both hands in her jacket pockets. "Tell me now how I was a sacrificial lamb."

"Let's go inside—"

"*Now!*"

She could practically smell his frustration. He wasn't used to not being in charge. Good.

"I thought"—he took a deep breath—"I thought I needed to get laid. I told you why."

"Because your self-esteem had been ravaged." She snorted. "Probably another lie."

Pain flashed in his eyes. "No. That was the truth."

"Then that's the only thing you were truthful about," she said softly, regretting the hurt she'd caused him, and then furious that she cared. Mouth twisted in anger, she spat, "You still used me."

Thrusting his fingers through his hair, he chuckled bitterly. "Isn't that a little hypocritical to say?"

"What are you talking about?"

"You used me, too." An edge of impatience sharpened his voice. "You used my reputation as a playboy to make it okay to have a purely sexual relationship. You used my fame to parade me in front of your classmates to show them you're worth something. You know, glass houses and all that."

Fury—and guilt—slashed at her like a million fiery little whips. "At least I was honest about it. You've lied about just about everything. About knowing Damon. About announcing the competition. About the interviews and late-night talk shows."

He frowned, the shadows from the lights overhead creating hollows that deepened his scowl. "I have no idea what you're talking about."

"You are unbelievable. Do you ever stop lying?" She glared at him, trying to ignore her breaking heart. "Go to hell. And leave me alone."

He said something, but she shut him out, turned him off like a song she hated on the radio. She started to resume her course for the parking lot, but it occurred to her that she was allowing him to chase her away. No more. Her heart had broken, but not her spirit. Never again would any man walk all over her spirit.

Raising her chin stubbornly, she brushed past him and headed for her room. And maybe if she was lucky, she'd see Damon. She had a fist that was itching to connect with his nose.

Sean let her go. She was too angry to listen and he'd only make things worse if he pushed. It was bad enough that he'd allowed his own temper to flare, especially given that she had every right to be upset with him, and not the other way around.

As he drove to his cabin, he tried to think of ways to make

Larissa Ione

it up to her, to make her understand what had happened. He couldn't come up with anything. Especially since he had no idea where the interviews-and-talk-show thing had come from.

The drive took forever, but when he finally arrived, the dark emptiness almost made him wish he'd taken even longer to drive. Being alone in his home had never bothered him before, but Robyn had changed all that. He couldn't look at his couch without seeing her there. He couldn't walk into the kitchen without picturing her smiling at him from the table. And he dreaded going upstairs to his bedroom.

Grumpy and depressed, he kicked off his boots and called to Norbert, who popped up from where he'd been sleeping on the couch. Sean petted the furball until, out of the corner of his eye, he saw the light flashing on his answering machine. His heart skipped a few beats. It was Robyn. It had to be.

He pushed the button and tapped his fingers on the table until the sound of his agent's voice made his stomach drop all the way to his feet. He listened to Samantha outline her plans to put him back into the spotlight—the interviews, the Letterman gig. Now he knew what Robyn had been talking about; she'd been here when Samantha called. No amount of cursing could even begin to express his emotions, but damned if he didn't try.

Norbert rubbed against his shin, and Sean bent down to pet the cat. "I'm an idiot, Norby."

Norbert agreed with a solemn meow.

"You couldn't have argued a little, you fleabag?"

Norbert stalked away, tail flicking. Sean let out a guilty sigh and fetched some treats from the kitchen. As he fed the cat he berated himself some more.

He'd probably lost Robyn for good. The one person who had ever given him a rush greater than any competition win. The one person outside his mother and sisters who had ever treated him like he was more than an empty-headed athlete. Somehow, he had to fix this.

He dropped a handful of treats on the floor and hurried to the phone, where he dialed Robyn's room. A female voice answered and his gut churned.

"Robyn?"

"Karen."

He winced. "This is Sean."

"Jerk."

She obviously knew what had happened. "I don't suppose Robyn is there?"

"Even if she was, she wouldn't talk to you."

"Karen—"

"Leave her alone. She doesn't need to listen to more of your lies. You used her. You tricked her. Not even Damon hurt her like that."

Being put into a category with Damon—no, worse than Damon—made him ill. "I know I hurt her. But I need to explain. I want to make it up to her."

She said nothing.

"Please."

She heaved a loud sigh. "I don't think you can. What you did was pretty harsh."

"I know."

"Worse than harsh."

"Yes, I deserve to die. Will you help me?"

Karen sighed again. "I'm going to regret this, I'm sure, but if you're serious, if you really want to get her back, it'll take something huge. Just so you know."

"Huge."

"Really huge."

"Right. Thanks, Karen. I appreciate it."

He hung up the phone and fetched a beer from the fridge. Huge. What the hell did that mean? What could he do? Somehow, he had to convince Robyn that they belonged together no matter how public his life became. Heck, with her radio background and his up-and-coming TV career, they could develop something big together, something they could share.

Unwilling to accept any form of defeat, he crawled into bed, wishing she was here to warm the sheets for him but feeling excited about tomorrow. First he'd announce the ski competition, and then he'd find Robyn and win her over. How, he had no idea. But he knew why.

If he didn't get Robyn back, all the fame and fortune in the world meant nothing.

Chapter Fourteen

Robyn tried not to rub her puffy, red eyes as she drove from Hausfreunde to the high school, where she'd participate in the auction set-up. It figured that the one day she needed to look good was the day she looked like a listless, sunken-eyed zombie following a night of crying on Karen's shoulder.

After she'd fled to her room following the confrontation with Sean, she and Karen had ordered room service that included all of the desserts on the menu. Even though Robyn had resisted gobbling up every last bite, guilt had set in. Guilt that she'd allowed someone to affect her so badly that she'd run to food for the first time in years. It was a measure of just how deeply Sean had ingrained himself into her soul, and a measure of just how stupid she'd been to allow it to happen.

Making matters worse, she'd been so furious with both Sean and herself that she'd gone to Damon's room and pounded on his door, wanting desperately to tear him apart with her bare hands. Fortunately, he hadn't been there, but even if he had, he most likely would have slammed the door in her face. He loathed confrontations, which was probably why he'd asked Sean to keep her busy in the first place. Confrontations led to anger, and anger led to Robyn not doing favors such as setting up *Rolling Stone* interviews.

Yes, she had him figured out. He wanted time to worm his way back into her good graces, and if that failed, he probably planned to wait until she was desperate for a job and at that point, he'd dangle one in front of her—a reward to be had only if she arranged the interview.

Still angry, she'd gone back to her room, only to learn that Sean had called, wanting to see her again. For what reason, she had no idea. The only explanation that made sense was that his competitive nature wouldn't allow him to lose something—even something he didn't want.

He'd called again this morning. The pain of hearing his voice had been excruciating, had pierced her incredible anger long enough for her to listen to what he had to say, that he wanted to meet with her before the ski competition.

Bad move, mentioning the competition. She'd told him where he could shove his invitation, and after she hung up, she'd taken off, blood boiling and nerves rattling, to the bakery.

The bakery that smelled of pastries and chocolate and warm walnuts and hot coffee. The bakery she'd loved all her life but that had also been a dangerous comfort for her. All that food and all her weaknesses had combined to make for a volatile mixture.

This morning, though, she fought the urge to binge. She'd settled for a cup of coffee and some self-liberating therapy. First, she'd called Brad to warn him that Damon might use her name to finagle an interview—and Brad, after hearing what Damon had done to her, had made clear that there would be no interview. She almost felt bad for her ex. Almost. Next, she'd dug into the dough, helping the staff create the daily specials. The time spent at the bakery had helped her think, and when her mother arrived to work, they'd had a long talk. By the time Robyn left the shop, she'd known what she had to do.

Now she just had to make it through the auction.

She trained her eyes on the high school a couple of blocks ahead. It had been remodeled to blend in with the newer, prestigious homes that had taken over the neighborhood, and it no longer resembled anything close to the ugly, squat prison building she remembered.

Far from it, in fact. An enormous party tent had been set up on the snow-patchy lawn adjacent to the gym, and strategically placed four-bulb Portofino lights and colorful paper lanterns added to the glitzy, festive atmosphere. Her classmates had spared no expense, had even added a red carpet that stretched from the parking lot to the tent entrance, and outdoor heaters lined the pathway.

Swallowing a wave of nervous nausea, she turned into the parking lot, which had already filled with vehicles. With only three hours to go until the auction began, classmates were scrambling to finish setting up, and she would have to let them know she was going to emcee.

She parked near the gymnasium and hurried across the lawn, her high-heeled boots crunching in the patches of snow. Her skirt, a calf-length emerald wrap, swished in the crisp air, periodically letting cold drafts fan across her legs as she walked past the larger items to be auctioned. Rafts, motor scooters and canoes had been displayed outside the tent, and as she approached, she mentally calculated possible bids, hoping the ads she'd placed in the newspapers and on the radio attracted enough guests to drive up the bid prices. With any luck, the fact that they hadn't been able to announce a celebrity auctioneer wouldn't result in a huge loss.

She slipped into the tent, where the morning sun had warmed the air enough that the heaters had been turned off. Robyn shrugged out of her coat and plucked her nametag out of a basket near the entrance. As she fastened it to her blouse, she sorted through the dozens of classmates until she found Linda near the buffet table that would soon be heavy with cuisine from several pricey delis. The other woman was instructing two former band-class members on where to place two locally donated oil paintings.

"Linda. It's Robyn," she said, after the men had lugged their cargo away.

Linda's eyes flared and dropped to Robyn's nametag as if needing proof of her identity, and then she settled into a comfortable smile. Linda had never been overly friendly to her, but she'd never been rude, either.

"It's good to see you. We've talked so much over the phone I feel like we're friends."

Sure, now that I'm thin. Smiling politely, Robyn nodded. "Did a shipment arrive from Los Angeles? Should have been a box from—"

"From GeeWiz," Linda interrupted, sounding a touch awed. "He sent several boxes. How did you arrange that? It's wonderful!" She gestured toward the back of the tent to a top-of-the-line karaoke machine that had been placed on a pedestal near the center of the stage with some of the more expensive items to be auctioned. "And he sent a videotape addressed to you. The note says to play it when the auction starts. We set up television monitors so people can watch."

Robyn bit down on a groan. George possessed a twisted sense of humor, so no telling what he'd put on that tape. She'd be wise to screen it before she played it in front of a crowd.

"Now, let's introduce you to everyone and let them know this is your baby."

Robyn gave a panicked shake of her head. "Uh, no, that's okay—"

"Don't be shy."

Linda took her arm and dragged her toward the stage. To Robyn's horror, Linda stepped up on the platform and grabbed the microphone.

"Everyone? If I could get your attention?" Linda gestured to Robyn, who wondered if she could find a hole to crawl into. A nice cold one to counter the heat in her face. "You may or may not remember our head auction coordinator, Robyn Montgomery, but here she is. She's going to make sure that this is the biggest money-raiser this school has ever seen!"

Applause followed, and Robyn smiled weakly as she raised a shaky hand to wave at the ocean of stunned faces.

Linda cleared her throat. "If you've read the bio pamphlets you know Robyn is a successful music director at one of the country's leading radio stations. So she's got some *very* prestigious contacts. In fact, she arranged for video jockey GeeWiz to send autographed items from some of the hottest pop stars."

More applause. More heat in her face.

"She's also arranged for a celebrity emcee."

Robyn's heart seized. It just...stopped. Her throat closed up, cutting off her breath, and she looked at Linda, shaking her head wildly, waving her hands to stop. Linda frowned and spoke into the mic again.

"Robyn is a little shy. Just a moment." She covered the mic with her hand and bent close enough for Robyn to smell the other woman's designer perfume. "What's wrong? You got an emcee, right?"

"No," she said on a groan. "I told you my emcee cancelled."

"But I thought you were getting another one!"

"I thought I could." She lowered her voice more because

people had gathered around, curious. "It didn't work out."

"You're kidding," Linda breathed. "What do you plan to do?"

"I'll handle it."

"Handle what?" Gigi's voice carried loudly from behind her and Robyn ground her teeth.

"Nothing."

"We don't have an emcee," Linda said.

Gigi's face lit up. "Really."

"We have an emcee," Robyn said. "Me."

"Oh, this is precious." Gigi climbed up on stage and snagged the mic from Linda. "Everyone, listen up. We have a special surprise today. Our own Robyn Montgomery is going to emcee the auction." She made a theatric, sweeping gesture with her arm. "Should be fabulous."

This time there was no applause. Lots and lots of dead silence, but no applause. Robyn stood there like a complete idiot.

This was *not* turning out at all like she'd planned.

✳ ✳ ✳

"So, do you miss this?" Jason Freeman, Sean's fellow commentator, gestured at the French skier who just blew across the finish line.

Sean peered down at the racer from his position in the tiny elevated booth near the base of the run and considered his answer carefully since his words would go on air. "I miss the racing, but I don't miss the practice."

Jason, a former Olympic medalist himself, nodded, jiggling his head-mic. "I hear you there. But practice is what gets you to the Olympics, and Owen Keaton, who is up now for Canada, is on the fast track to the next winter games."

And that quickly, they were back to giving the viewers a running commentary. Sean had effortlessly settled into the routine, which had been a huge relief. He hadn't tripped over his own words, hadn't forgotten a name or any of the lingo.

Even better, he wasn't the slightest bit jealous of the skiers, which surprised him, given that he'd felt a distant burning in his gut every day for the last two years when he thought about what he lost, and what he'd love to have back.

But right now, what he wanted back was Robyn.

He couldn't stop thinking about her, couldn't stop hoping for a miracle. He had to find a way to win. Had to find a way to slide across the finish line with a record time on the clock. When a competition win had mattered, he'd squeaked by with a hundredth of a second to spare, and he'd do it again.

But how?

They went to commercial and the door to the announcer room whispered open. Damon strutted in, leaving snow tracks on the sisal carpet.

"You guys are doing a fantastic job." He clapped Sean on the shoulder. "As soon as you wrap up, head to the party at the Rendez-Vous."

He winked as though he was merely making a suggestion to attend the party of the year at the state's most exclusive resort, but the man had issued a command. "A lot of important people will be there. Everyone who is anyone in the biz."

Sean shook his head. The last thing he wanted to do was schmooze with a bunch of people he didn't know or like.

And what. The. Hell. Something was wrong, because they were exactly the people with whom he needed to schmooze if he wanted to spark a successful career full of cameras and sports. So what if the new career took away from his time on the slopes and his job as an EMT? The medical job was just busywork anyway.

He looked out the window at the couples who snuggled against the cold and at the skiers who'd finished their runs and now waited for the race results. Behind the crowd, ambulance crews stood by in case a skier or bystander needed medical attention.

No doubt the medics were bored out of their gourds as they waited for a call that would get the blood pumping, that would define the very reason they worked and that made all the hours of tedium worthwhile. Sean knew exactly how they felt, and as scenes from every crazy, hectic, exciting call flashed through his head, he remembered the satisfaction he took from making a difference in the lives of people who needed him. He thought about how skiing treacherous terrain in search of lost skiers shot him full of adrenaline, and how just snuggling with Robyn felt like a jolt of life itself.

And he knew. He didn't want to go to a party. He wanted to work. As an EMT. He wanted to ski. As a patroller. He wanted to snuggle. With Robyn.

And damn it, he wanted it now. He stood and looked Damon straight in the eye. "I'm not going to the party."

Damon's greasy smile slid off his face. "The station execs will be there. If you don't show up, I can't guarantee your job."

"Right. The job." He glanced at a cameraman nearby, who signaled five seconds to on-air. "Tell you what. You keep the job. You keep your condescending attitude and your threats. I'll keep my sanity. And Robyn."

Jason, who seemed to be holding back a snicker, tugged Sean's sleeve and mouthed "on-air".

With a shrug at a visibly agitated Damon, Sean returned to his seat and commented on the last skier, an Italian, who took the championship.

Sean glanced behind him and saw that at some point Damon had left. Too bad. He wouldn't be around to hear what was coming next. Well, he'd hear, but by the time he charged up to the booth, Sean would be long gone.

Jason, talking into his headset, looked at Sean. "Well, that concludes the competition. Stick around for the post-game analysis, and tune in tomorrow for the world snowboard championships. Sean Trenton, thank you for being with us."

Sean smiled. "My pleasure." He looked down at the scripted thank-yous he'd been given to read. "I'd like to thank all the locals for their hospitality, and special thanks to Drake Motors, Martin Hotels and Tristan Family Restaurants for their sponsorship."

He shoved the script away. "And I'd also like to thank Albert McKinney High School for their support of Ski-Do, a non-profit organization that helps put underprivileged kids on the slopes. In fact, the school is hosting a charity auction this afternoon, and bids will go to a good cause. I'll be there, and we'll see who else I can round up. Hope to see you."

Jason looked horrified. He glanced at the off-air indicator light and rubbed the back of his neck. "Sean, buddy, you just broke a cardinal rule. No personal promotion on air. You screwed yourself."

Grinning, Sean pushed away from the desk. "No way, man. I think I just saved myself."

Robyn stood on the stage, knees shaking, using the narrow podium as a shield. It was time for the auction to start, and here she was, unable to speak to the audience in the half-empty tent.

By past standards, the turnout wasn't bad. By her standards, attendance was a failure. The local radio stations were supposed to have advertised the auction several times daily for the last week, but she'd learned that none had. Damon had struck again, part of his "crushing her", she guessed. Somehow, he'd managed to cancel the announcements.

Fortunately, he'd neglected to contact the newspapers, which was probably the only reason people had shown up at all. Well, that wasn't quite true. When Linda informed her of the radio fiasco, she'd called the stations and asked for quick mentions. The DJs had been happy to oblige, so the auction had gotten some good last-minute promotion. Still, Damon had probably done a lot of damage by canceling several days worth of ads.

So now she stood all alone on the stage while guests submitted private bids on the merchandise displayed in the gymnasium and tents, and here she was, trying to think of ways to entertain them and convince them to bid. She'd managed a "hello" and a "welcome to the auction". Really impressive.

The two television monitors mounted in the tent's rear corners showed her terrified face, and to her horror, it was true that the camera added ten pounds. She looked positively bloated and distorted.

Static blackened the screen, and then George's face appeared. She nearly groaned. She'd forgotten to watch the tape he sent, but Linda hadn't forgotten to play it. Great. Who knew what he'd say?

"Hey, bidders! Welcome to the auction. Your coordinator asked me to emcee, and since she's a close friend of mine, I wanted to do it. Unfortunately, I can't get out of this crazy town of Los Angeles." He winked, and some of the women in the audience giggled. "But I do have something for you. It's nothing as special as the woman who put all this together, but I had to try. Meet some of my other friends."

Robyn watched, as stunned as the guests, as George introduced several pop stars, all of whom addressed the audience and encouraged them to bid for a worthy cause. By the time the tape had finished ten minutes later, tears stung her eyes and she felt warm inside. George's contribution had taken more thought and care than anyone had shown her in a long time. Anyone other than Sean, anyway.

Forcibly shoving any thoughts of Sean away, she put her lips to the mic, confident for the first time today that she could do this.

"Ladies and gentlemen. I know I thanked you, but I'll be honest. I was terrified and hardly knew what I was saying. Now I mean it; thank you for coming. Your bids will help children who otherwise might never learn the joys of skiing, and more importantly, who might never have been given the opportunity to develop skills and friendships and confidence that'll last a lifetime."

She looked out over the crowd that seemed considerably happier after the video. Behind them, what had been a trickle of people wandering inside became a flood so huge that the band-class guys had to open up the tent's two sidewalls. Where had they come from?

Confused but pleased, she reached for the list of merchandise to be auctioned, unhooked the mic from its stand and held it close to her mouth. "And now, let's go over some of the items..."

Her voice trailed away. She blinked, unsure if she was really seeing what she thought she saw. A group of men and women, all wearing jackets corresponding to their nations' ski teams, spilled inside the tent. In their arms, loads of ski equipment, and in their lead...

Sean.

Her knees went weak. Her heart somersaulted. She felt dizzy, so dizzy. The man she both hated and loved was walking toward her. He wore an easy smile, but his golden eyes glowed with intensity as they caught and held hers.

Tracking her open-mouthed stare, people turned, and immediately a low rumble of voices stirred the crowd, which parted to allow the athletes through.

A wave of people followed him inside, and even before he came to a complete stop at the base of the stage in front of her, the tent had filled to capacity. Still more people gathered outside. How had he done this? Though she had no concrete proof he was responsible for the sudden increase in visitors, she knew nevertheless.

"What's going on?" Janice whispered from the back of the stage and Robyn shook her head, unable to speak and as confused as the other woman.

"Can I have the mic for a second?" Sean asked.

Numb, she nodded and handed it to him as he hopped up on the stage. He looked magnificent in jeans faded in all the right stress points and a black ski-patrol logo sweatshirt, and his vibrant expression only made him more irresistible.

"Hey, everyone!" he began, and several people in the crowd shouted return greetings, stirred by the sudden excitement in the air. "Robyn Montgomery, a very special friend, asked me to emcee today, but I had another obligation. I feel like a heel, and

I'm trying to make it up to her. I brought some friends, members of several US and international ski teams, and they were all kind enough to donate autographed equipment for auction. They'll be happy to meet everyone, sign autographs and pose for photos, hams that they are." Laughter swept the assembly in a wave and Sean grinned, completely at home on the stage.

"I'd be grateful if you all would help me wriggle back into Robyn's good graces by buying everything and paying a ton of money for it." More laughter and Sean shot her a smile she felt all the way to her heart. "Now, I'm going to see how else I can help, so if you'll take a look around, place some bids, someone will be back to talk to you in a minute."

A buzz ran through the crowd, and it seemed as though a renewed sense of excitement sent people hurrying to the items up for auction. Fingers flew, pencils scratched out numbers on the item bid forms.

Robyn cast a glance at a group of her classmates standing near the buffet table, all of whom were watching her with approving smiles. All of them except Gigi, who scowled until Janice elbowed her in the ribs. Gigi rolled her eyes and sent a reluctant nod in Robyn's direction.

Sean jumped off the stage and pulled her toward the rear of the platform where the audio and video equipment afforded them a little privacy. "Hi," he said.

For lack of a better response, she replied, "Hi."

"I'm sorry."

For that, she had no words. She wasn't sure how she felt about all that had happened, the lies, the betrayal, but what he'd just done had definitely confused the hell out of her.

People started to migrate toward them, so he took her hand and drew her outside, which was nearly as crowded as inside the tent. He looked around and then gave her hand a gentle tug. "I have an idea."

She didn't even think to protest as he led her into the gym, where they weaved through the throng of bidders before ducking into the school hall.

When the door closed, he faced her and jammed his fingers through his hair. "I'm going to be completely honest with you, okay?" She nodded, a quip about him not knowing the meaning of the word stuck on her tongue because she was still too stunned by what he'd just done, and he continued. "The day I met you, I was trolling for women. Any woman. To get laid."

"This...is supposed to make me feel better?"

He quirked a smile and squeezed her hand. "Todd wanted me to go for something easy, a sure thing to get me past my issues. Two years ago, that's what I went for. Fast, easy women who liked to party as much as I did. But the other day in the Moose...for some reason that type of woman didn't appeal to me. I didn't know what was wrong."

He took a deep breath and fixed his intense gaze on hers. "And then I saw you. You're the exact opposite of everything I'd ever liked. You're beautiful, but you're *real*. You're intelligent. And strong. And resourceful."

He reached out and twirled a lock of hair around his finger, and it took every ounce of restraint she had not to sink her cheek into his caress. "I love that your hair is dark and you aren't six-feet tall. I love that you have curves. And brains. And I think what really hooked me is the fact that I wanted you, but you didn't want me. Do you know how refreshing that is?"

She knew all too well what it felt like to want someone when they didn't want you back, and the last word she'd use for the feeling was *refreshing*. Humiliating, excruciating, mortifying. But not refreshing.

"This is all very flattering, but I'm still not sure what your point is."

He smiled that disarming smile of his and cupped her cheek in exactly the way she'd wanted him to. "I wasn't sure *why* someone as different as you appealed to me that day. But now I know. Deep down, I didn't want a quick lay. I didn't want a fling. Robyn, I wanted a relationship. I still do. Yes, my goal when I met you was to get you in the sack, but it turned into something else before that ever happened."

Her heart believed him, what with the way it hammered away inside her chest like it was trying to break out and get to him. Her brain, though...it needed a little more convincing.

"But?"

He looked down at his feet before looking back up. "But not before I made the deal with Damon."

"So you're admitting you lied to me to get me into bed."

"Sort of," he said soberly. "I mean, I didn't tell you about the announcing job because I wasn't sure how it would turn out. And I wasn't sure my agent would be able to score anything else." He twitched a shoulder in a half-hearted shrug. "I figured that since we were just going to be doing the fling thing it wouldn't matter. And the deal with Damon, well, I honestly thought I was helping. He said if I kept you busy he'd make sure you had a job."

This all sounded so reasonable, so not the evil plan she'd thought it had been. "Still, I'm sure it didn't hurt that he was willing to give you a job."

His shoulders slumped as though the weight of the truth was too much to bear. "No, his job offer didn't hurt. I think I was fooling myself into thinking it was about you, but it was about me. At least, it was about me until I started falling for you. Then it became about you real fast."

Emotion clogged her throat and she had to swallow several times before asking, "You fell for me? Even after you saw that picture?"

"Did you think less of me after you found out what I'd lost to cancer?"

She shook her head. "Of course not. But that's different."

"How? It's all external. Stretch marks, weight, missing body parts. I don't care what's on the outside. For the first time, I want what's inside. I love you, Robyn." His voice broke, and splotches of pink colored his cheeks. "I don't want all the fame and fortune if it means losing you."

"Sean. I-I don't know what to say. You'd really be willing to give up all that for me?"

He nodded. "I already have. I told Damon to take a hike, that I wasn't going to his party to schmooze with the execs for a job. I don't want it. I want to patrol. And I want to come home to you."

She slapped a hand over her quivering mouth as tears spilled from her eyes. What he was saying, what he was willing to do...it was too much.

"I can't let you do that," she murmured from behind her palm. "I can't be responsible for you giving all that up for me."

"Sweetheart, don't you get it? I want to give it up. I want to be with you. I realized today how much more important it is to be happy than it is to be famous. And you make me happy. I know you need to get a job somewhere, but I can transfer to a nearby ski area and ambulance company. We might still have a bit of distance between us, but—"

Gathering his hand in both of hers, she pulled him closer, until she could smell his woodsy aftershave. "No. I'm moving here."

"What?"

"I worked out a deal to buy Hausfreunde from my parents. I'm going to run it. I have all these plans! Remember the rosemary cheddar loaves? You gave me a great idea. I'm going to bake them as bread bowls. And I have some thoughts on eventually expanding the business..." She trailed off at the stunned expression on his face that turned to radiant pleasure.

"Then please, please say we have a shot. I'm so sorry about everything. Please say you forgive me. Give me another chance."

As much as she wanted all of this to be over, it wasn't. There was still an issue between them. "I can only forgive you if you do the same for me."

"Robyn, I'm the one who screwed up. Not you."

She shook her head and gripped his hand tighter. "No, you were spot on when you said I was using you. And just because I was upfront about it doesn't make it right."

"It's okay—"

"No. It's not. I treated you like you were nothing but a famous face. I didn't look beyond your name and accomplishments, and that's something that I, of all people, should know better than to do." She chewed on her bottom lip for a moment. "You deserved better than that. I'm so very sorry. Can you ever forgive me?"

"You shouldn't even have to ask," he said in a voice so rough with emotion that a sob formed in her own throat. "Of course I forgive you. Can you do the same?"

Warmth swelled in her heart, and she threw her arms around him. "Yes, yes and yes! I forgive you, and I love you, Sean Trenton."

He kissed her hard, as though his very life depended on it. His lips crushed hers, and his tongue swept inside, robbing her of her breath and sending electric tingles over her skin and through her bloodstream. The hall was empty, and he took advantage of that, pushing her back against the lockers, winding his fingers through her hair as he held her close.

As always, her body responded to him like they'd been lovers for years. Her breasts tightened, her thighs clenched as heat and moisture built between them. The hard ridge of his erection behind the seam of his fly pressing into her belly told her that he was as affected by the kiss as she was.

"Sean," she whispered against his cheek, "I know where there's an empty room."

He groaned and pulled back. "As much as I want to make love to you right now, we can't. I have an auction to emcee."

What a wonderful man. She smiled and shook her head. "You don't have to—"

"Yes, I do. I let you down, and I'm going to make it up to you."

"You already have. The equipment, the ski teams..." She frowned. "And how did you get all the people here?"

"I announced your auction during the competition," he said with a sly smile.

Oh, but he was a gem of a man. Damon had managed to cancel her radio announcements, but the announcement had still gone out on his television network during his time and on his dime. What delicious irony.

"I can't thank you enough." She arched an eyebrow at him. "I also can't let you emcee. I'm going to do it. I want to do it. More importantly, I need to do it, just like I needed to buy Hausfreunde to prove I'm stronger than I've always believed. I can find a better use for you."

"If you're sure."

"I'm sure. And afterward, I'm going to show you how grateful I am." She kissed him, a brief but intense kiss that left no doubt as to how she'd demonstrate her gratitude.

Breathlessly, he took her hand to lead her toward the gym doors. "And I'm going to show you how much I love you."

She couldn't wait. But she stopped him just short of the doors. "I don't suppose you could show me something else, too?"

"And what would that be?"

She chewed the inside of her cheek for a moment and then blurted, "Ever heard of a game called hide-the-mitten?"

A slow, secret smile curved his luscious mouth. "Oh, baby, I know it. And the best part?" He leaned down, brushed his lips across her cheek and whispered into her ear, "In that game, there are only winners."

She glanced down the long, empty hall and smiled. Here in the high school that had been little more than a giant torture chamber for her, Robyn the Troll had found happiness. She most definitely was a winner.

About the Author

Larissa Ione, an Air Force veteran, has been a meteorologist, EMT and professional dog trainer, often all at the same time. Yet she never gave up on writing fiction, and is lucky enough to now write full time, which is a blessing given her husband's military career.

She lives a nomadic lifestyle with her U.S. Coast Guard husband and son, currently residing in Virginia, though she considers the Pacific Northwest to be home.

To learn more about Larissa, please visit www.LarissaIone.com. Send an email to Larissa at larissa@larissaione.com or join her Yahoo! group to join in the fun with other readers and authors as well as Larissa! http://groups.yahoo.com/group/writeminded_readers.

Reunited by their teenage son's possible involvement in a murder...old passions and new needs are destined to explode.

His Ordinary Life
© *2007 Linda Winfree*

Del Calvert has spent his life in quiet desperation, trying to meet everyone's expectations and feeling like he never quite measured up. From his teens, Barb was everything he wanted and needed, but knowing he wasn't enough for her drove him out of the marriage.

Barbara Calvert is afraid to need anyone—especially the soon-to-be ex-husband she still loves. She's reluctant to fall under his seductive spell of love and security once more.

But when their son's secrets threaten his life, everything changes. Del must help his son as unseen and threatening forces move ever closer, putting the entire family at risk. And along the way, he hopes to convince Barbara to give him one more chance to win back the wonderful, ordinary life he didn't appreciate until it was gone.

Available now in ebook and print from Samhain Publishing.

Enjoy the following excerpt from His Ordinary Life...

Leaning up, Barbara covered his mouth with hers, cutting off his words, and he was lost, drowning in sensations he'd starved for the last few months.

She cradled his face, her lips teasing the corner of his. The clean essence of her surrounded him, a mingling of citrus, soap and woman. When she eased her tongue over his bottom lip, he hardened. A groan rumbled from deep in his throat.

"Barb," he whispered, and as his mouth parted, she darted her tongue inside. At the taste of her, his knees threatened to give. He reached for her, gripping her waist and pulling her closer. Her body aligned with his, fit him with the same perfection as always. "God, I've missed you."

He muttered the words into her mouth, sliding his hands lower to cup her bottom and lift her against him. She moaned and wound her legs around his thighs, the counter supporting her weight. Holding his shoulders, she urged him even closer and sucked his lower lip into her mouth, nipping him lightly. The sensation of pleasure-pain shot to his groin and he rocked into her.

With a rough laugh, he rested his palms on the counter on either side of her. Her head tilted back under his kisses, she tugged his shirt from his jeans. "Take it off."

"Baby, you know where this is headed," he murmured between kisses, her fingers leaving trails of fire on his skin. "Are you sure?"

"Take it *off*, Del." She shoved the shirt up, helping him shrug out of it. Once it hit the floor, she fanned her hands over his chest, shaping the muscles, tracing the line of his ribcage. She ran a single finger along the scar bisecting his left pec, and he closed his eyes. Over the years, she'd done the same thing countless times, but this once, the simple caress brought tears to his eyes. She pressed a kiss there and he moaned, swaying closer. This wasn't really happening. In a second, he'd wake up and find it was simply another dream.

He bent his head, seeking the curve of her neck with his mouth, tangling his fingers in the plush robe, pushing the edges aside so he could find her curves. A breathy sigh escaping her, she arched into his touch. The pulsing fire in him burned hotter. He trailed his lips to the hollow of her throat, her pulse beating against his mouth.

He cupped her breasts, her skin still damp from the shower, and nuzzled her shoulder while he brushed his thumbs across her tightening nipples. Her head fell back, a little moan purring in her throat. God, everything she did was the hottest thing he'd ever experienced.

"You're so beautiful." He muttered the words against her skin. "Sexy." His mouth caressed the slope of her cleavage. "Perfect."

"Hardly." The word escaped her on a husky laugh. She clutched his hair and massaged his scalp. He swallowed, a groan building in him. "Childbirth and nursing three babies don't add up to perfect."

"My babies." He circled a hardened nipple with his tongue, drowning in her gasp of pleasure. "*Our* babies." He flicked his thumbnail over her dampened skin. "You've always been perfect to me."

Using her hold on his hair, she pulled his head up and took his mouth again in the slowest, sexiest kiss of his life. With his palms, he worshipped the line of her body—her breasts, the indentation of her waist, the flare of her hips. The muscles of her stomach jumped against his hand when he stroked his knuckles across her smooth skin. The blonde curls below were soft and damp, and when his fingers found her, she moaned into his mouth. Already hot and slick, she pushed into his touch.

She gripped his shoulders and slid her mouth from his. "Oh, you feel so good."

He buried his face against her neck, kissing her there, loving the feel of her rubbing his shoulders and back. She knew what he liked—strong, firm caresses, long sweeping strokes of her fingers, the occasional sting of her teeth and nails on him—and he was burning up with what she did to him.

She skimmed his sides with her short nails and ventured beneath the waistband of his jeans, almost but not quite touching him where he needed it most. She brushed him with one finger and he bucked, groaning.

"Del," she whispered, and he lifted his head. Gripping the counter's edge with white-knuckled hands, he stared at the wanton picture of her, damp hair tousled, eyes dilated with passion, robe open exposing rounded breasts with rosy, hard nipples, his tan dark against her paler skin. She didn't smile and a hard knot settled in his chest. Lord, she was going to tell him to stop. The dream was over.

She touched him, curving her hands to his rib cage, thumbs rubbing down the spasming muscles of his stomach, stopping at his jeans. With a slow motion and a teasing smile, she popped the button loose on his fly. He was going to explode, then and there from nothing more than that minx-like smirk and the anticipation of her touching him. Even slower, she slid down his zipper. The jeans slipped on his hips, and one fingertip crept into the band of his briefs.

Explode, hell. He was going to die from the expectancy, but, Lord, what a way to spend his last moments. She pushed the briefs down, stroking him, and he gasped, knees ready to buckle. "Baby, you're killing me."

Still caressing him, she wrapped her legs around his hips once more. She kissed him, dancing her tongue along his lips.

"I want you," she moaned into his mouth. "Inside me."

Sliding his hands under her thighs, he lifted her against him, ready to carry her off to bed. "No." She tightened her legs around him, positioning him at the entrance to her hot, wet core. "Here. Right now."

GREAT
CHEAP
FUN

Discover eBooks!

THE FASTEST WAY TO GET THE HOTTEST NAMES

Get your favorite authors on your favorite reader, long before they're out in print! Ebooks from Samhain go wherever you go, and work with whatever you carry—Palm, PDF, Mobi, and more.